TRACY WHITWELL

Love Button

Copyright © 2023 by Tracy Whitwell

All rights reserved. No part of this publication may be reproduced, stored or transmitted in any form or by any means, electronic, mechanical, photocopying, recording, scanning, or otherwise without written permission from the publisher. It is illegal to copy this book, post it to a website, or distribute it by any other means without permission.

First edition

*This book was professionally typeset on Reedsy.
Find out more at reedsy.com*

For every woman who thinks it's over, it just isn't okay?
Be free, be you, be naughty.

Contents

PROLOGUE	1
CHAPTER ONE	5
CHAPTER TWO	8
CHAPTER THREE	14
CHAPTER FOUR	20
CHAPTER FIVE	25
CHAPTER SIX	35
CHAPTER SEVEN	40
CHAPTER EIGHT	47
CHAPTER NINE	56
CHAPTER TEN	67
CHAPTER ELEVEN	69
CHAPTER TWELVE	79
CHAPTER THIRTEEN	84
CHAPTER FOURTEEN	89
CHAPTER FIFTEEN	93
CHAPTER SIXTEEN	99
CHAPTER SEVENTEEN	113
CHAPTER EIGHTEEN	121
CHAPTER NINETEEN	127
CHAPTER TWENTY	134
CHAPTER TWENTY-ONE	140
CHAPTER TWENTY TWO	144
CHAPTER TWENTY THREE	149

CHAPTER TWENTY-FOUR	153
CHAPTER TWENTY-FIVE	164
CHAPTER TWENTY SIX	174
CHAPTER TWENTY SEVEN	182
CHAPTER TWENTY-EIGHT	185
CHAPTER TWENTY-NINE	193
CHAPTER THIRTY	198
CHAPTER THIRTY-ONE	214
CHAPTER THIRTY-TWO	216
CHAPTER THIRTY THREE	221
CHAPTER THIRTY-FOUR	225
CHAPTER THIRTY-FIVE	230
CHAPTER THIRTY-SIX	233
CHAPTER THIRTY-SEVEN	238
CHAPTER THIRTY-EIGHT	247
CHAPTER THIRTY-NINE	252

PROLOGUE

I have mascara in my eyes.

I have been crying for twenty-two minutes and I can't seem to stop.

About an hour ago I was quite happily pootling about in Ikea; then I went into their toilets and did the pregnancy test I'd been putting off for two weeks. I'd just ordered a burnt orange chair. Tommi likes neutral colours but our new house, which we only moved into a week ago, is all neutrals, like a clinic, and I like vibrancy. He can't win all of the time, so the cream chair he asked for became an orange chair – all happy and new and asking for attention. Then I went to the loo, feeling brave because I'd done something rebellious, and peed on the stick that'd been in a box in my bag since last Thursday.

And two blue lines appeared.

We haven't been trying for a baby and I'm usually very careful. But it seems that something has gone wrong. Well, wrong in that I've had itchy nipples for ages and I cried at a dog-food commercial this morning when I don't even have a dog. Maybe not wrong in the case of an actual pregnancy because I am thirty-three and in amongst my shock and fear there was a germ of excitement. When I saw the two blue lines

I didn't cry. What I did do was drop my purse down the toilet by accident so I was forced to fish it out quickly and wrap it in toilet paper and wash diluted pee off my shaking hands.

No, I didn't cry until well after I'd veered home in my almost clapped out green Corsa and tried to call Tommi and he'd not answered.

He was probably in a meeting at work, I thought. So I decided to email him. I went to his new office-space upstairs, which is supposed to be a bedroom but he's a graphic designer and needs to work at home sometimes and anyway we have other spare bedrooms. Two more. (Too many if you ask me.) I don't usually go near his stuff but this was an emergency. When I pressed the 'on' button on his PC it was already 'on'. It lit up immediately and went straight to his hotmail account which he hadn't logged out of. He'd come up to bed well after midnight and full of wine last night so I guessed he'd forgotten to log out.

This didn't make me cry either. I don't care if he comes upstairs late and full of wine. I like wine. I'm often full of wine myself. But what I saw on the screen concerned me. Emails, loads of them, from our mate Tess. Well, his mate Tess. Who's going out with Bri. Alias Roger Ramjet. He loves extreme sports and she's one of those women who manages to be girly and funny and tough all at the same time. Like a dinky, funky, wind-up bunny. Unlike me – I'm curvy and ungainly and a goof and not tough in the slightest.

Anyway. I read one of these emails, quickly followed by the rest. Then I started to cry.

An early example…

'**… I've tried so hard not to think about what happened that night but it was so good. We fit – I knew we would.**

PROLOGUE

I have never felt anything like this with Bri and I know it's wrong but I don't care... Just tell me when you can get away again and this time we can spend more time making each other happy... I love our little secret... Your little Tasty Tess x'

Before I cried I nearly vommed. Tasty bloody Tess. What a terrible pet-name. Since the first email I read, according to her missives, they'd been 'doing it' a lot and Tasty Tess was still loving it. What a shitbag.

I cried and am still crying twenty-two minutes later and while I'm crying, I'm wondering how a woman can do this to another woman. She's sat and chatted to me about personal things, held my hair back when I puked after a dicky oyster (Tommi can't 'do' illness of any kind, it totally freaks him out) and basically pretended to like me while stealing my boyfriend.

Tommi. My tall, grey-eyed, messy-haired boyfriend. We've been together nearly eight years. We're a long-term item. Why would he do this when we've just bought this massive, stupid house together? I stare around at the cream-coloured walls and organic-looking carpet, wave upon wave of nausea hitting me as I realise that he has been 'at it' with someone else, a beautiful little back-stabber, and I will probably be storming out of this house before I even settle into it. I can't stay with a cheat. I can't. In the past when he's been inattentive or huffy or just plain infantile and selfish, I have thought of leaving. When he's gone out 'with the lads' and not come back until next day, I have told him I've had enough and he's talked me round. He's suddenly become a handsome, contrite angel and wrapped his arms around me and rested his chin on my head and told me I am everything to him. But now I've found out I'm pregnant. I can't have a baby with a baby of a man.

A BABY.

If I ever manage to stop crying I shall call his office and leave a message. If he's not here to talk to me within the hour I will pack and leave. I can't do this. Not with a cheat.

CHAPTER ONE

Morning is never my favourite time, never has been. But this morning is especially annoying because Tommi has a half day off. He rarely takes time off but there was a birthday party at his work last night and he thought he might like to rest, just like he does on the weekends. Stupidly, I got it into my head that he might take this opportunity to accompany his five-year-old son to school. Maybe give him breakfast, talk to him about his upcoming day, force him into his uniform and walk the ten minutes to his school in an act of father-son bonding that so rarely happens on a weekday. And give me an almost unheard of lie-in.

But, obviously, that can't happen because Tommi is in a coma. Well, he would be, wouldn't he. Not one to consider the consequences of his actions or the future, Tommi stumbled in at two-thirty this morning, stinking of whisky, as wobbly as a new-born fawn and so confused he ran a bath. He then got in it because 'he'd run it now' and I, eventually, fell asleep again after lobbing my flip-flop at his gormless head and missing. The only upside to the situation was that he was too drink-fuddled to reach out and grab me, in the mistaken belief that he was being 'alluring'. These days I'm usually so worn down, I can't think of a single circumstance in which having sex would be preferable to being asleep. Or drinking wine. Or reading a book, or watching a film, or staring into space. My head is so full of domestic concerns, work stress and boy-child nonsense that there is literally no space left for anything as demanding as having sex. My fantasies now revolve around sitting in silence and contentment with nobody asking anything of me for a whole half hour.

As I glare at my dead-looking partner through one scrunched up eye, watching him drool into the pillow as he marinates in his very own whisky fug, I hear the sound of curtains opening in a toy-filled room close by, and turn to the door just in time to spot a messy head peering round at me. Barney steps in and grins, makes a weird hand gesture that he probably just made up and jumps up and down twice. His pyjama bottoms are too short and have aliens all over them, he is wearing a vest that's gone a bit grey in the wash and he looks adorable. I reach out my arm and he runs to me. I hug him and smooch his warm boy-neck then he splats a wet kiss on my face and commences a noisy game of aeroplanes around the room. Without opening his eyes, Tommi wraps a pillow around his head.

Weary or not, this obviously means I must throw on my long cardie and play dutiful mummy. I will have to get my boy fed, ready and at school by nine o'clock, jump on a bus then a tube and be at work by ten. My old boss let me have the working hours of ten till five so I could do the school run in the morning and be home for six to relieve the babysitter. My new boss, Harry, finds this infuriating and doesn't care that I'm brilliant at my job. To him I'm simply 'the part-timer'. And today won't be any different because that lazy sod next

CHAPTER ONE

to me isn't getting up any time soon and I won't be getting to work any earlier or any less stressed than usual.

Tommi. I hate you.

CHAPTER TWO

I am panting painfully as I sprint into our hallway with the 'family montage' cork-board and sticky smudges that I forgot to wipe off the expensive cream wallpaper. The stroll to school was surprisingly lovely, Barney did not fight me once. He held my hand and we played I-spy. The sun was out and his hair was all springy, and when I hugged him goodbye he smelled of fruity shampoo. I should have gone straight to the tube station after dispensing him into the incredibly dull but reliable hands of Miss Benson (who looks like a gerbil) but that was when something went wrong. Something always bloody goes wrong. Suddenly, I discovered I'd forgotten my phone. No mobile phone would mean no number for my childminder and many other essentials, so I had to hotfoot it home.

In an attempt at damage limitation and stress management I've decided to get a cab to work just this once, like I'm Simon Cowell or something. It'll be expensive but I'll just close my eyes and try not to think of bankruptcy. Bankruptcy is never far from my thoughts considering how hard it is keeping up the payments on this stupid massive house and the related bills and sundries, plus that bloody Eco car that Tommi wouldn't buy secondhand so we have to pay an astronomical fee for

CHAPTER TWO

each month. I hate that car of his. It's all to make him look cool and we should have got something much cheaper. I call it The Little Shit. He knows I do but he doesn't care.

I creep back upstairs and Tommi is still flat-out in a cloud of stale alcohol. I open the window a crack to let out the fumes. I've not seen him like this for a while. I hope he's set his alarm because I'm not ringing him from work to get him up, the bone-idle so and so. I find my phone on the dressing table. As I grab it I spot Tommi's iPhone on the floor next to his discarded jeans. It probably has very little juice in it. Being Mrs Stepford Wife, I can't just leave it there, even though I'd quite like it to go flat and cause him inconvenience. So I pick it up and plug it into his charger. As I do, it buzzes in my hand like a rogue locust. I nearly jump out of my skin.

A little envelope sign pops up with the name 'Em' and the beginning of a message:

Hey hunny. Loved the taste of your beautiful...

I can't help frowning. A rather over-familiar text. The only 'Em' I can think of is Emma at Tommi's work. I've met her a few times, she's lanky and student with a loud laugh, long blonde hair and jeans that hang off her tiny bum. I've never really found much to say to her. I didn't think Tommi had anything in common with her either. Before I can stop myself I press the little envelope. Still in the back of my mind I believe the text will end with 'Margaritas' or 'chocolate orange' (he loves chocolate oranges. He would live on them if I let him). But it doesn't. There are just three more words:

cock last night.

I look again. Because that can't be right. That would imply that some stupid, dull, braying bitch had her mouth on my boyfriend's penis last night. (Unless they were eating a male chicken together.) I stare at him, lying there as sweet as a cherub. A cherub with stubble. Then I look back at the phone. My scalp grows hot and tight. Tommi is still cute, with stickyup hair and slate-grey eyes that have females melting. Women still giggle when he speaks, and most people seem to find him very funny. But for me, parenthood has taken its toll and over the past few years I've become less and less interested in his jokes. I mean, when you've heard one you've heard them all, right?

Without thinking much what I'm doing I snap open the blinds and drag off the duvet. He's naked. Floppy naked. I aim my tattered Ugg and kick him hard in the shin. His leg is hanging out of the bed and I kick it again. I wish I was wearing something pointier. The sleeping giant yelps and an eye opens.

He's done it again. After five years of bringing up a child I thought he might have grown up a bit. Fuck knows, I've had to. Ever since I looked in the mirror and truly admitted that my figure was not 'snapping back' like Chrissy Teigen or Posh Spice or any of those other monied, sneaky, surgical miracles. Ever since I acknowledged, miserably, that I was still softer and bigger, plus I was not allowed to do what I wanted anymore, plus I was not the carefree career woman I'd been before. I was a housewife. I was my mother. I was suddenly infinitely older and fatter and I wouldn't be 'me' ever again. Thirty nine is not old but lately I've fucking felt it.

'Enjoy your night out, did you?'

My voice sounds five octaves higher than usual and there's a whooshing in my ears. He blinks up at me and struggles to drag himself out of unconsciousness. Almost comically gropes about and knocks his glasses off the bedside table

CHAPTER TWO

before grabbing and gulping a mouthful of stone-cold coffee, no doubt to lubricate a mouth full of dry pebbles, and winces.

'What?'

'Just thought you must have had fun, what with getting a blow job and all that.'

This time the wince is more pronounced.

'WHAT? What are you…?'

Before he can finish, I thrust the phone in his face. He pats quickly about on the floor then shoves on his little oblong specs. Seeing the message he goes the colour of a church candle. That and the hangover sweat is not an attractive mix. I remember he went a similar colour last time he was caught out.

'Fuck. Fuck, Alice, she's just messing around…'

I throw the phone at him and it cracks off his knuckle. He yelps then jumps off the other side of the bed as I try to kick him again.

'Alice!'

He's not used to me kicking him. I want to kick his head off.

'You liar. You're the one who's messing around. I'm assuming this is the Em I've met? Why does she have your private number?'

'For work.'

'Well, that's the funniest work message I've ever read. Ha ha. What a hoot. Weird, she didn't strike me as the comedic type when I met her.'

'Jesus.'

It takes nothing to get me shouty mad these days. Too much noise in the house, a fridge door not properly closed, socks on the sofa… anything can send me off like a badly primed grenade. But this is different. I want to rip his face off, I want blood.

'Did you shag her?'

'What? No! It's...'

He pulls on his jeans over his naked backside and flaccid-looking man bits. Then it fully registers. He's not wearing pants. Of course he isn't, he had a bath. A bath! Now it all makes sense. Here was I thinking he was just being a dippy drunk, when actually he was washing off the evidence.

'I've been stupid, Alice. A stupid idiot. I got very drunk last night and she, well Emma, she...'

'What? Orally raped you? Sucked your penis behind your back while you were chatting to the office temp?'

'NO! Stop.'

He approaches and tries to hug me. Wrap me in those long arms. He always rests his chin on my head. Well, other Tommi did, the one I trusted. Well, mostly trusted. This Tommi is not getting anywhere near me. This Tommi who promised never to let me down again but just did. She sucked his cock. I start flapping my arms at him, trying to slap him. I am unnerved by this violence I feel. I've had post-natal depression and he's been getting his cock sucked.

He jumps backwards to avoid a bunch of slaps.

'We got talking. About everything. Sometimes it's hard, you know. To talk, me and you. So we talked and then - '

'Then what?'

'She wasn't drunk, she said she'd drive me home. She stopped around the corner and...'

'She sucked you off in the car? Nice. Did you kiss first? Were you kissing?'

'I... well yes, a bit, but I felt queasy then she...'

'Don't give me 'she', you obviously weren't protesting much.

CHAPTER TWO

'No.'

He can't look me in the eye.

'Did you two attempt to shag when you were in her car around the corner from our house?'

'No! I was pissed. I was not in any position to have sex. And why are you talking like this? It's like you're enjoying it. Please Alice, let's sit down and discuss it properly. We've got to talk about us, she's got nothing to do with us.'

I suddenly feel chilly inside.

'Do you like her?'

He blinks. Takes a breath.

'I did. Until now. She likes me, she laughs at my jokes. I don't piss her off all of the time. But that doesn't mean...'

It's a strange thing about men. They are always totally honest at the wrong time. Or maybe it's the right time. I've heard enough and the fight goes out of me. I just want to get out of here.

'I'm going to work. I don't want you here tonight.'

He reaches out a hand and touches my shoulder.

'Please Alice. This isn't fair. I've been an idiot but...'

'But what?'

'Well it hasn't exactly been hearts and flowers around here recently, has it? Not for a long time. Every time we have sex it's like you're doing it under sufferance. Sometimes I just want to, you know, feel loved. Feel carefree. I'm sure you do too. But I shouldn't have done that last night, that was a drunken fuck-up.'

I can't believe he's justifying this. And not-so-subtly blaming me. He promised.

'I have to go to work.'

CHAPTER THREE

'Hello, can I speak to Emma, please?'

I'm in a cab. I'm feeling this mixture of fury and nausea. The driver is either not listening or making a grand job of pretending not to.

'Emma Bailey speaking.'

That nasal voice. I picture her rabbity face. Stupid fucking Rabbit Face. For a moment I don't know what to say. Then I do.

'Hello Emma, how are you? It's Alice here. Tommi's wife. Apparently you had a grand old time sucking his cock last night. Apparently he was too drunk to go any further though.'

There is a silence on the line. Then she speaks. I really dislike her voice. Like a honking goose.

'Do you think it's appropriate calling me at work? Not very classy is it?'

My God, is she having a laugh?

'About as classy as the text you just sent him, you fucking bimbo.'

'Well, if you saw it, you know. Good.'

I can imagine red spots coming up on her cheeks. Dry tongue licking at those big front teeth. I can imagine she doesn't like confrontation, but she's trying to be Mrs Clever right now. Another bit of me can just as easily imagine that she couldn't give a shit.

'Does it matter to you ONE BIT that he's been with me for nearly fourteen years and we have a child together?'

She lowers her voice, suddenly sounding less like a goose and more like a wasp.

'Does it matter to you that you're crushing him, you frigid cow? He's a lovely, funny, intelligent man and he needs someone who treats him right. Why should you hold a cosh over him just because you trapped him with a kid?'

There speaks a woman who has never given birth. Just you wait Rabbit Face.

'Oh my God, you horrible little witch. You have no idea what you're talking about.'

Now there's a sneer in her voice.

'Little witch that Tommi adores. He loves our lunch dates at the pub, it's the only time he gets to talk. You've got no-one to blame but yourself.'

She slams the phone down. She puts the phone down on me. What the?

Suddenly I'm sobbing. Big baby yowling. Amazingly the cabbie says nothing, just passes a tissue over his shoulder. For the last five minutes of the drive I cry uncontrollably. Partly because my man has had his cock sucked by someone else when he promised 'never again' and partly because I have been a frigid cow. My relationship mojo ran off a long time ago. And he told her. Confided in her. They've been having lunch dates. I mean, everyone fancies other people, right? But it doesn't mean they act on it. Especially when they already did before.

Tommi, you shit.

The cabbie pulls up outside my office. He swerves into a disabled parking space and three drivers behind beep furiously at suddenly having to slow down. Now that we're here I have to pull myself together, because if I show weakness in front of Harry Percival I will be torn to shreds. I pay the cabbie, wipe my face, powder my cheeks and take a deep breath.

'No-one's worth it love.'

The cabbie's parting shot, as he shoots his car out in front of a mightily pissed off bus driver.

By the time I walk into my workplace, I am to the outside world, I hope, my usual determinedly professional, potentially sarcastic self. But undeniably late. I get to my desk just as Harry stalks in, leather satchel under his arm, grim determination in his eye. He doesn't say anything so either he's late too or he's been in a meeting somewhere.

The first time I saw Harry I thought he was attractive with his public-schoolboy dirty-blond hair, turquoise eyes and rugger-bugger physique. But then he showed himself to be an arrogant twat and due to me needing my job I had to bite my tongue and get on with it. One day I will deck him in public. If he messes with me today then he might live to regret it. Lucky for him, he goes straight to his office, slamming the door behind him.

Elen, the girl at the desk opposite rolls her eyes. Elen is a little, kooky-looking chick with a huge wardrobe of elderly women's dresses that she jazzes up with crazy footwear and belts. She's good fun and the only person in this office that I don't find irritating. Every week she asks me to come out on Friday night and every week I say no. She thinks I spend too much time in the house. She's probably right, but how

CHAPTER THREE

much more tired would I be when Barney wakes up if I stayed out late drinking? I'm better off staying up late in the house, drinking. Saves a cab fare at least.

I'm feeling peculiar in my head and stomach. I may cry again. Elen spots it, of course.

'What's up, Buggy, you've gone a funny colour?'

She calls me 'Buggy' as in 'Buggy Botherer'. She can't understand why anyone would have children. She doesn't say it in a nasty way though, it's sort-of affectionate because she thinks Barney is the cutest kid she's ever seen and gives me toy monsters for him sometimes.

'I'm okay. Just had an argument with Tommi this morning. Could have done with some extra sleep.'

What the hell is going to happen? If I only think of the next hour ahead I'll maybe get through the day. Just the next hour.

'No Buggy, you don't need sleep, you need fun. Fun, fun, fun. You need to come out on Friday. There's a little gang of us going to The Dog. Please come out, we can have a dance. You've got great taste for an oldie.'

She says this in jest but sometimes I wish she wouldn't. I'm thirty-nine and I feel fifty-nine. Especially today. At first I think she's said 'we're going to the dogs' which would sum up my life perfectly. But then I catch on. The Dog in Camden. She mentions it often. She loves that place.

'If I'm so old, why would you subject me to a whole night of being surrounded by drunken infants?'

'Because you're not irredeemably old. And you're funny. I think you'd love it.'

I try to smile. Just so I don't alarm her by bursting into tears and crawling around on the office floor like a kicked poodle. At that moment my phone rings. It's Tommi. I stop the call. A minute later my desk phone rings. I can't ignore it as it'll look suspicious. I pick up and it's him.

'Alice, are you okay? We need to talk. I love you.'

'Not while I'm at work.'

'I'm so sorry about this. I'm so sorry you found out that way. She shouldn't have sent that message… I would have spoken to you, you know. I wouldn't have deceived you.'

'You already did. This is number two.'

'Please. Alice. We need to sort this out.'

I breathe in. Yoga breathing, they call it. Taking air to your diaphragm. Calms anxiety attacks. I had a few of those a couple of years after Barney was born.'

'Tommi. Can we talk about this later? I just want to get through the day.'

He suddenly sounds hopeful.

'Of course, darlin'. I'll see you at home.'

I don't want to see him at home. Well, maybe I do but I'm gutted and I can't discuss it right now. Belle, the office gossip, will be tuning in and she has ears like a bat.

'Okay. Just for a while. I meant what I said, though.'

I click off.

I'm so tired. He says 'home' like it means the same as it did yesterday. Elen is staring at me.

'What's going on?'

'Elen, I need to go for a walk. If any of these nosy bastards ask, can you tell them I've got cramps, my PMT has got me ready to kill and I'm buying major painkillers?'

'Course.'

'Bye.'

My head spins with questions as I walk through the fume-filled city-centre air. How could he do this again? Is it my

CHAPTER THREE

fault? Is it because I look like shit? Are we going to split up?

There's a tiny park six minutes from the office. When I say park I mean a five-foot by five-foot square of scrubby grass with a bench on it. Dedicated to 'Lois. A lovely lady'. I sit next to a dozing tramp, kick a kebab wrapper and sob for a bit. This afternoon he'll be at work with Em. How could he do this to me?

I hate him.

CHAPTER FOUR

Facing Tommi at home isn't much fun. Barney, as always, is joyous when Daddy gets in from work; but I'm now sure that I can't sleep in the same house as him. Not yet. I give Barney a custard cream, tell him to play on his bike in the garden, then ask Tommi for a week's break. This is strange, as usually when we argue or something goes wrong, I cling to him and try to make it better. But not tonight. My brain is tussling with a lot of things. He has pre-empted this, another first, and informs me that Talia and Geoff have offered him a room in their house for a few days, if he should need it. They are our mutual friends, though I inherited them from him. Talia's a little older than me and a very successful architect. That's how come they live in a massive house in Hampstead with a nanny, their two children and a goat called Mungo, who has his own kennel. Geoff is a session guitarist and really cool. I am miffed. I shouldn't be but I feel like they're taking sides already and I'm scared of what Tommi's said to them. I wonder if he knows this is how I'll feel and is hoping I'll let him stay here instead.

Keeping an eye on Barney through the kitchen window, I shun all of Tommi's attempts to hug me or touch me. This is what he did last time, the day I found out I was pregnant. He seduced and comforted me. He made love to me so tenderly I surrendered. This time I'm not bloody having it.

'Alice. I've been weak.'

'Too right you have.'

When he stares down at the table he looks the same age as Barney.

Tears are running down my face but they're just as much tears of humiliation that I trusted him, as tears of sadness that he's 'strayed' again.

'But I didn't have sex with her. I promise.

'A blow job is sex, Tommi.'

'No. No, it isn't. You saw me last night, I was so drunk, I hardly knew what was going on. I've been a fool but it's not like before. Before, I was stroking my own ego by getting too close to an old friend when I was a bit scared of commitment. An old friend who told me she was in love with me. And I've kept my promise ever since, haven't I? We didn't see them again, did we?'

'No.'

Tess sent me a couple of texts in the month after I found the emails. To my eternal shame I told Bri; called him that same night in a whirl of hormonal righteousness and told him he'd better ask his girlfriend who she'd been 'fooling around with'. He apologised, the poor lad. Said he had no idea. Apparently he was heartbroken and dumped Tess immediately. When she contacted me, asking to 'put some things straight' I told her in no uncertain terms to lose my phone number and never bother us again. So she did and as far as I know she moved to Scotland. Good riddance.

'This time I was drunk and Em was completely sober. It's not an excuse but it's different. I didn't see it coming, I thought she was my friend. It really really won't happen again. We've just got to sort our own shit out, Alice. This is about us and Barney.'

His voice has taken on a wheedling tone that I don't like but he's right about one thing. It's been a long time since I actually wanted sex with him. It's been something I've done as rarely as possible with my eyes and mind closed. Mostly because almost everything he's done and said over the past few years has annoyed me. And this shit has to be talked about or that's it for our relationship.

'Can I just have time to process this on my own, Tommi? Before we talk about anything else I have to get over the shock. I just need space.'

He departs with a sports bag of belongings after Barney is tucked up in bed.

I cry a little as he goes. He gives me a hug. I promise we'll talk very soon. At least he'll have company at their house. At worst he can climb into the kennel and cuddle Mungo. When he's gone, I pour a large glass of Prosecco (I know, I should drink it from a flute but they're too small and this is a bloody emergency) and I call my mate Suze. She's married to my other mate Smithy and I'm always scared there'll be problems if I call him first because he used to fancy me years ago. But in the end it doesn't matter because once I tell her something awful has happened, he starts chipping in in the background and she barks

'Skype!'

They look funny on the screen. He's already on at least his second glass of wine, I can tell by his red-stained teeth. He's losing his hair more rapidly nowadays but he's still handsome. She looks knackered, but her wavy mane is well coiffed and she keeps shooting him disapproving sideways glances. Once I explain what has happened, as far as I know it, he butts in before Suze can offer me anything measured by way of a response.

'Redress the balance.'

'Sorry Smithy?"

'You can't talk about this properly with Tommi until you've redressed the balance. Get your pride back. Otherwise you'll just be pissed off and hate him.'

(I never told them about the 'first time'. I told no-one. I wonder if he'd have said this same thing when I was pregnant.)

Suze glares at him like he's a maniac. Then she looks into the camera at me.

'That'll get you nowhere, Alice. Just because men are weak when it comes to sex, we don't have to be.'

He nudges her so she falls off her chair and out of shot.

'Al. We're fucking idiots, us men, but we don't mean it! For whatever reason he needed an ego boost and 'poof!' he messed up. I'm telling you now, go and get a bit of attention yourself. Get your ego boost and remember who you were before. Then you can talk to him man to man, so to speak.'

'I can't do that!'

'Yes, you fucking can. You've been bored for ages. You said yourself, you've never been the housewife type. Shake it up a bit and for gawd's sake DON'T TELL HIM. This is for you. A cheeky present to yourself. That's what I would do.'

Suze pushes herself back into shot and punches him in the arm.

'Alice, don't listen to him. He's not a woman. And if he shagged someone else I'd bloody stab him.'

He begins to laugh.

'No you wouldn't… You looooooove me.'

Suze is infuriated by Smithy twenty times a day. But she loves him implicitly. They couldn't have kids but you wouldn't be able to drive a sheet of A4 between them, they're so tight.

'Alice, listen to me. You guys haven't had it easy. Having Barney was difficult for you. The amount of times you've told me that you're tired of everything. Maybe Tommi's picked up on that and felt rejected? Maybe it is just a stupid mistake and he is actually sorry?'

I know what she's saying and I'm trying to listen, but the male of the species has won this particular round. Smithy's right, I have been bored and pissed off for ages. I swallow down the rest of my drink.

'I don't know what I'd do without you guys. Thank you so much for your help, you've really made me feel better. I need to rest my head now.'

And redress the balance.

'And have another glass of this, of course.'

Suze gives me a reassuring glance, Smithy just winks.

'Drink as much as you need, Al. And get yourself out there.'

Suze slaps his arm.

'Stop saying that, you idiot. Love you, Alice.'

'Love you too, Suze. And you Smithy, you drunken bugger.'

'Big kiss to Barney.'

Then they're gone.

Redress the balance.

CHAPTER FIVE

It's only 8.55 a.m. and I have walked into a madhouse. Work is in uproar. Apart from arrogant Harry, who's only been here six months, and my little friend Elen, who's still basically a trainee and does what I tell her, there are four other workers at Benham Design. Most notable is Belle, who's fifty-six years old, loves metallic eyeliner which I think is supposed to be 'retro-chic' but just makes her look insane and who has impressive marionette lines permanently creased into her troweled-on foundation. Belle is an old-school gossip, who fishes for information left, right and centre and has a finely tuned radar for other people's shenanigans. She must be the most bored woman in existence at home to be so excessively nosy in the workplace, but you'd never know because all she does is harp on about how well her kids are doing at college and how good her short, bald husband is at building new houses and selling them.

My question about that is, if he's so good and they're so minted, why does she work? I don't think answering phones and greeting clients was her calling in life, so I can only assume she would have nobody to spout off at or interfere with if she didn't have a job.

I reckon a big clue to her personality is how far her kids have gone, university-wise. One's in Fife, the other in Ireland. It doesn't take a genius to work out that she must irritate her own progeny. I think Belle should be replaced by someone less appalling, but she's worked here a long time and she doesn't do anything bad enough, apart from being an irritating meddler, to merit her getting sacked. The other three in our fabulous workforce are Jim, who's geeky, tongue-tied and keeps himself to himself, Jemma who's beige, dippy, just married and who goes for lunch with Belle every day, and Hassan who does most of the work, apart from me, and is snipey and sometimes amusing. Hassan is Pakistani, quite young and smoothly posh, with an impressive overbite and a penchant for the kind of clothes that Wham wore in the 1980s. He talks a lot about pulling girls, but I think he's gay. Not that I'll ever find out now because he's apparently had a nervous breakdown, out of the blue, and run off to Australia. Consequently, Harry's chief designer is out of the picture and we have three big deadlines to meet in the next fortnight.

Belle is like a wind-up Duracell bunny when I arrive, already in conspiracy overdrive, conjecturing all over the place about what has happened to Hassan. Her theory so far is that his father has discovered some kind of perversion in his son's personality and has shipped him off to a sex clinic in Arizona. You couldn't make this up. Well actually, she just did, so you could. I can't prevent a twinge of envy that Hass has been able to fuck off without a single responsibility. I reckon he hasn't had a nervous breakdown at all; he's just decided to go elsewhere and work somewhere better for more money and is taking a holiday first.

My head hurts. Too much fizz and too little sleep last night.

CHAPTER FIVE

While I'm cranking up my computer and sorting out my desk I glance up and find Elen staring at me.

'You look terrible, Buggy.'

'Thank you, Elen.'

'What's going on?'

'Nothing. I told you. Been having a few arguments with Tommi and...'

I try to trail off but she's still looking at me, waiting for the next bit.

'You know. Well, you don't, you've never stayed with anyone for more than four months.'

She gasps. 'You two haven't split up have you?'

She doesn't say it loud but it doesn't matter. Bat-ears hears it anyway. In three seconds flat, Belle is at my side.

'You awright, darlin'? Having a bit of trouble at home?'

'No, Belle, not really. Elen just misconstrued.'

'I know what it's like, you know? Young kiddie, arguing about every little thing, the magic all gone. It can be blinkin' awful.'

She's glaring at me like a hungry hawk and to my eternal shame my eyes well up. OH GOD, THAT'S ALL I NEED. Of course she notices and strikes in triumph. Gobbles me up like a cowering field-mouse.

'Aw no! Sorry love, did I upset you? You see, that's relationships. You should come out for a glass of wine at lunchtime. Get it off your chest, talk to Auntie Belle.'

She has her boney arm around me. I stare menacingly at Elen who mouths 'sorry'.

'Thank you, Belle. Honestly, I'm just tired, everything's fine.'

She gives me a reassuring pat on the arm, the type that says 'you stay in denial, love. Who am I to make things harder for you?'.

When she's gone I shake my head at Elen who pulls her chair closer to my desk.

'I'm so sorry, Alice. Really. Eurgh. Auntie Belle? Auntie Bellend more like. Please come out. Friday's going to be such fun. You can come to my place beforehand and we can have drinks and chats. It'll be great. We can even listen to a bit of your 'vintage' music! Pleasey please?'

'I don't know. I'd have to ask Tommi to babysit. Or get my mum to travel down.'

Actually, if Tommi's with Barney he can't be with 'her' can he? The cock-sucker. What if he's not keeping his distance from her at work like he said he would? But he's pathetically desperate to please me right now, isn't he? And a night out can't be any worse than another night in, can it?

On Fridays, Tommi and I usually have a takeaway and watch something on Freeview. Or he goes out for a pint and I watch something I actually like, or read a book. He also has boys' nights out on Thursdays so he gets plenty of time off. It's probably about time I had some 'fun'. I can just take ear plugs and get rat-arsed.

While I'm mustering the wherewithal to text Tommi, Harry emerges from his office and calls me in. He looks awful. Harry's father-in-law owns this company. He owns lots of companies, but he charged Harry with running this one as we hadn't been making enough of a profit. That's mostly because designing office interiors and corporate spaces is not so in-demand as it was when the country actually had some money. We're just not as lucrative as we once were and we don't pull in the big-hitter clients, so I think there's every chance this place will close down. Apparently Harry's wife, the big boss's daughter, is a stunner. I've not met her, I've only met her dad, Charles Benham. He was at the work 'do' last year. He was white haired and tanned, with the most expensive-looking watch in the world. You'd think Harry was a lucky sod for having such great connections but he doesn't look like he's feeling lucky right now.

'Hassan's gone, Alice. Disappeared. We've got to pull together here. If we're going to meet those deadlines on time we've all got to work our arses off.'

'Okay. But why are you saying that like I don't work my arse off already?'

'You can't be showing up last and leaving first every night anymore.'

'I have a child, Harry. I do the hours I'm paid for, the hours I agreed with David.'

This again. The heat is rising in my chest. I have to contain it.

'David's not here anymore and I didn't agree to anything. Why should you having a child be my problem?'

Must contain it.

'My having a child is hardly a 'problem'. I still do more than my fair share of the work.'

'Well, just think how much more work you'd get done if you stayed for a whole working day!'

Oh dear. He just went too far. The steam pushes my lid off and my volume goes to eleven. I have never let rip at Harry before, but I've truly had enough.

'How dare you! I work hard for this place. Jim and Hassan and I have always more than met our targets and if it wasn't for us you wouldn't have a job yourself. Maybe you should have been nicer to Hass and he wouldn't have gone! And just to clarify, if you call my Barney a 'problem' once more I will rip your fucking throat out. Now fire me. Fire me or treat me right, you arrogant shit!'

I'm shaking. So is he, I note with some satisfaction. I stand up and stalk through an office of open mouths, straight down the stairs and out into the street.

My euphoria doesn't last long. I'm probably sacked. I don't know where to go so I head for Soho. Café Bohème will be open and I need a drink. My phone pings as I walk. It's a text from Elen:

You fucking rule

I'm fucking unemployed.

Soho is lovely at this time of day. It's quite sunny so I sit at the open window and order a cappuccino and a flute of house fizz. I'm shaking again. Food is as interesting to me as a plate of rubber right now. I've had virtually nothing since I saw that text on Tommi's phone. A couple of slices of toast, maybe. That's probably why I'm behaving like this. No food but plenty of drink is making me rather emotional. I call Tommi as my drinks arrive. He picks up immediately, but is lowering his voice.

'Alice?'

'Alice, indeed.'

'Are you okay?'

'Yes. I am. Well, I had a row with Harry.'

'That git giving you trouble again?'

It's nice to hear his voice. It's hard to believe that there's anything wrong between us, we know each other so well. Well, we did.

'Yeah. It's fine though, it's nothing. He just wants me to work more hours. We're having a bit of trouble at the office.'

CHAPTER FIVE

'Really? When does he want you to work?'

This is new.

'Probably on and off in the evenings over the next fortnight. Just to meet some deadlines. Hassan's left without giving notice.'

He pauses, then surprises the hell out of me.

'Well, what if I could get to Barney by six whenever you needed me, over the next fortnight? It's not that busy at work. As long as you don't mind me coming over.'

Now it makes sense.

He never hurries home usually, that's my job. But if it gets his foot back through the door when he's in the doghouse. Not that I can afford to be choosy about it.

'Okay. That would be great. I just have to make sure I still have a job first.'

'What?'

'I threatened to kill him.'

'You didn't!'

He begins to snicker down the phone and I snicker too. Moments like these stab me because we know each other so well. Then I hear a woman's voice on his end of the line. As his hand goes over the mouthpiece it all gets blurry and distorted for a moment. Then he's back, almost whispering and not snickering any more.

'Sorry Alice, they're calling me into a meeting. Just quickly, are you, erm... Are you still coming this weekend? I'm finishing early to get there for teatime.'

I have no idea what he's talking about. I scan my memory banks and draw a blank.

'Mum's birthday?'

GOD! It's Eva's sixty-fifth. A meal on Friday night and family barbecue all day Saturday. Shit. There's no way I can go.

'Tommi. I can't be dealing with family stuff right now, I am so sorry. But we've already got her gift, you can give it to her from all of us.'

'Right.'

His voice is tight.

'I'm really really sorry. Of course, you should still take Barney. I'll call her and tell her I have to work overtime or I have the plague or something.'

'Take him on my own?'

'Yes Tommi. I've taken him plenty of places on my own. Just pick him up from school and drive him to your mum's. He'll be over the moon to be with Nana and Gramps and his cousins for a couple of nights.'

'What will you be doing?'

'Dealing with this week's bombshell. Having a rest. Having a think. What does it matter?'

'I'll miss you.'

'We can talk about that when you come back.'

'Can we?'

'Yes we can. But don't pressure me. If you can't keep it together while I work this out, then you're not the man I thought you were.'

He already isn't. He's a stranger who had his cock in someone else's mouth and betrayed me again. And I miss him. But I won't tell him that.

'I'm sorry, Alice.'

'I know.'

He sounds very unsure. He always knows where I am and what I'm doing. I never really noticed that; I always thought I was the control freak. But he seems so insecure about me

CHAPTER FIVE

having some time to myself. Well, tough.

As I end the call, I notice a lady opposite me, strutting down the street. She's probably over forty but she doesn't scurry like me. I always seem to be scuttling like a frightened crab these days, trying to catch up with the rapidly retreating stilettos of life. She walks like she owns London. She's not overly dressed up, just a sassy looking blouse with jeans and wedges. Her hair is probably the same length as mine, but it has an expensive sheen and is well kept. She looks cool. I used to feel cool. The first sip of chilled fizz makes my head buzz. I alternate with sips of coffee. I must look crazy. Good. At least I'll seem interesting for a change.

I forlornly take in my outfit as I check out the departing backside of the lady in wedges. She's not a skinny little thing, she's quite big, and totally sexy. I wear so many layers, it's hard to tell if I have an arse. Or legs or ankles. Or even a neck. I am the furthest extreme of those women who wear the 'mummy uniform' at school. Not the young mums, who wear tight jeans and groovy little tops and sometimes even heels. The older ones who can't get their bellies to go back down after being inflated like zeppelins and who wear big pants with leggings and long sleeved 'mum' tops.

Another sip of fizz and I remember something. I reach into my big, carry-everything-I-own-in-the-world, faux-leather sack and rummage through receipts, stray packets of jelly snakes, toy cars, broken eyeshadows, body spray and my threadbare purse, until I find what I'm looking for. It's a flyer. There's a picture of a model with an asymmetric haircut on the front and the name of a hot-shot hair salon on it. Some doubtful-looking kitten of a girl with the milkiest skin in England passed it to me as I hurried to work this morning. It entitles me to £40 off a cut and colour, which would probably still leave me with at least two hundred quid to pay. These places are not cheap. But I remember hearing before, that if you're going through a crisis, a haircut can do wonders. And make no mistake, this is a bloody crisis.

So I call them and make an appointment for Friday lunchtime. If Barney's going away with his daddy and I'm already sacked, I may as well have a decent haircut while my life collapses around my ears. Hopefully they can't make me look any worse. I'll just have to get out the emergency credit card so Tommi doesn't know.

Because what he doesn't know can't hurt him, right?

CHAPTER SIX

I never go to fancy hairdressers. Years ago I did but not now. Money's always too tight. (Even though there are other expenses that bleed us dry, the one I really resent is The Little Shit. That car might be Eco-friendly but it's not bank-balance friendly. And I hardly ever get to drive it, seeing as Tommi takes it to work with him.)

I'd forgotten how nice these places are. There's just that air of expense. The shampoos are all posh and the stylists are 'hip'. Do people use that word now? I feel ridiculous and shabby in my old black work trousers with a long jumper and Uggs. A liquorish oblong with appalling hair. Everything I have worn for the past five years has been for comfort. But surely comfort doesn't have to look this shocking? I hand the assistant my coat. I swear she's looking at me sympathetically. But that could be paranoia; I always think people are looking at me like I'm a bag lady. If they look at all.

It occurs to me, as I'm putting on the smock, that apart from my functional work-gear, every piece of clothing I own is old enough to have had Barney's baby-vomit on it. And only half of it does up any more. Bigger belly, bigger boobs. Barney is obsessed with my breasts at the moment. He thinks they're toys. He's also been asking questions about why his daddy isn't at home this week. I've told him he's working late and leaving early, but that's not going to hold up for much longer. Barney is a smart boy. As I sit waiting for a consultation with the stylist, I'm hit with another wave of surprise that I'm still employed.

When I got back to the office on Wednesday, expecting to be sacked, Harry just nodded at me and said, 'Better now?' When I nodded back, he slunk into his office. There was quite a pile in my in-box and I figured he simply couldn't sack me when he has something to prove to his father-in-law and is already a man down.

Apart from Elen, who kept winking at me and shaking her head in admiring disbelief, everyone else left me to it. I don't know what they all said when I was in Soho, but they evidently concluded they should keep a wide berth. Even Belle left me alone. Eventually I went into Harry's office and told him I'd been out of order, shouting at him like that. Even though I didn't think I was out of order at all. And then I asked if I could take a half-day's leave on Friday afternoon to sort out a 'family matter'? Pushing it at the best of times. When he looked like he might protest I told him I could work extra hours over the next two weeks and I would do everything in my power to make sure all deadlines were met, not just mine but Hassan's. For the second time in a day I surprised him into silence. Then he said Friday would be fine. And he almost smiled. Smug shit.

The stylist is called Elaine. I think she's half Japanese. She has a smooth black crop and is wearing a vest top with harem pants; the kind of thing that would make me look like a clown. I'm feeling rather uncomfortable about all of this 'changing my hair' business until she offers me a glass of wine. I'm dumbfounded. Wine in a hair salon? So that's what you're paying for when you come to these swanky places. I totally approve. I ate a bowl of Barney's chocolate Weetos this morning so I've lined my stomach and I gratefully accept a large glass of white. Then she takes the pin out of my shaggy bun and begins to comb my hair out, just to look at it. It falls past my shoulders, is in no discernible style and the ends are lighter than the dark roots due to not having been cut for a whole year. She shakes her head and smiles.

'Someone needs a conditioning treatment.'

On the few occasions that I go out with Tommi and whenever I have to look semi-smart for work I use curling tongs on my hair to give it some body. The heat has murdered it.

'Sorry. I know. I've been so busy.'

'Don't be sorry, that's why you're here. You need a new style that can frame that lovely face."

Something about having a glass of wine in my hand, being in such a nice place and being told I have a 'lovely face' gets to me and I choke up.

'I don't have a lovely face but thank you."

'You do too, look at those cheekbones. Are you okay?"

I'm not about to use this little hairdressing beauty queen as my psychotherapist, so I drum up a smile.

'Sorry. Uber-shit week. Just ignore me.'

She grins. Teeth like pearls.

'Uber-shit week turns into super-hot hairstyle. Just you watch. Do you trust me to make you look fantastic?"

I pause. I don't know. 'Erm...'

'I won't cut loads off. Just above shoulder length, make it nice and shaggy. And I won't dye it purple or pink, scout's honour. I'll frame your face and bring out your eyes with the colour. You game?"

Why the hell not. I salute her with the glass.

'Go for it. And make it as vibrant as you like, I used to be a rocker you know!'

As she foils and heats and snips and rinses and conditions and snips again, I flick through a bunch of terrible magazines with pictures of perfection in them and made-up stories about people I'll never meet and don't care about. It's vacuous but it's also gloriously decadent and the head massage at the beginning seems to have lifted a ton of garbage from my shoulders. When she eventually says it's time to dry it, I've studiously avoided looking at what she's been doing. She takes out a large round brush and smiles at me.

'Here goes!'

After ten minutes I behold the finished article. She has cut it blunt just above my shoulders with a matching fringe. The indeterminate dry brown is now chocolate brown and there are shots of bronze and a couple of steaks of bright red running through it. As promised, the eyes that had looked a muddy colour to me, now seem brighter and have flecks of green, like they always used to when the sun shone. But then, this brightness of eye may also have something to do with the two glasses of Pinot Grigio I've just downed. Drying my hair with that brush has made it sleek and put body into it, it actually *bounces*. I hardly look like me. That's not a bad thing.

'It'll be easy to maintain. You just need one of these brushes, some colour-protect shampoo and a heat-protect serum. We stock all of them."

I'll bet they do.

'What do you think?"

CHAPTER SIX

I'm seeing the other things on my face that I wish she could have changed as well as my hair. The lines from my nose to my mouth, the less-than-tight jawline. But at least she's covered up my forehead with that heavy fringe and made me look less mumsy, so that's a bonus. I shake my head and watch it move. It's happy hair.

'I think I really like it.

'So you should. You look great.'

I don't care if it's her job to say that. For a second I believe it. I smile at myself. My face transforms when I smile. That's what Tommi always says. I pat her hand.

'You're brilliant."

She glows. Even gorgeous girls need a compliment, it seems. The cut and colour plus all of the products come to an extortionate amount of money. I add a tenner as a tip, close my eyes and hand over the credit card. It was worth it. As I exit the shop, I wonder how a session at the hairdresser's could possibly be so up-lifting. It's probably the novelty. And the fact that Tommi would kill me if he knew how much I just spent.

I need some water after all that wine. I wander towards a kiosk and pass an office window. I glance sideways at myself and am struck by two things. How much better my head looks and how crap everything else looks. The trousers, jumper, coat and flatties, all in dark colours. All melding into each another like a muddy river. I have got to sort this out. I take a deep breath and turn on my worn-out heel, towards a huge department store in the other direction. I have to get the credit card out once more. I am going out tonight and I literally haven't got a stitch to wear.

CHAPTER SEVEN

I'm late. Shopping took ages, considering how little I bought. Then getting back took forever because of a broken-down tube at Euston and then I fell asleep for two hours because of the daytime drinking and I woke up on the sofa, panicking, at six o'clock, feeling like I'd swallowed a mouthful of cat litter. It took two pints of water, two pieces of toast (one of which I left) and three quarters of an hour of faffing to get myself in order. Then I ordered a cab which evidently came via Belgium and, eventually, here I am, arriving at seven-thirty instead of seven o'clock. Elen doesn't even look like she's noticed. That's youth and 'all the time in the world' for you.

She gives me a big hug and leads me up a dingy staircase, through a nondescript front door and into fairyland. I fall in love on sight. This flat has fuchsia walls and aquamarine curtains, with Dali prints and Art Nouveau lamps. It's thrift-shop chic and it's the flat I would have loved to have lived in if I'd spent a few years on my own instead of settling down so quickly.

'Oh my God, Elen, I love this place.'

She beams.

'Thank you. And I love your hair! It looks fab.'

CHAPTER SEVEN

I run a hand through it.

'You think so?'

'Of course I do. It's all bouncy and glam! What do you want to drink?'

I brandish a chilled bottle of fizz and she claps her hands.

'Nice one!'

She's playing some kind of gypsy music in the background and I can't help a little jiggle as she goes off to the kitchen, returning almost immediately with wine glasses with sunflowers painted on them. I feel like I've gone to heaven. As she pours, I admire her outfit. A 1970s dress that hugs her curves well. Elen is quite short with rounded hips and tonight she's really used it to her advantage with a dress that clings in the right places, patterned flowery tights and platform shoes. She looks great. Young, daft and happy. Once she's poured and we've had a long slurp she sizes me up.

'Okay. So let me see you properly, please.'

I am more than a little self-conscious as I stand there in my new jeans, dress and boots. I find shopping for clothes totally horrific, though I did discover some black skinny jeans with a high waist which I really liked and bought. The thing is, though, I'm so under-confident about my shape these days that I couldn't buy a little top to go with them, and show my bum, so I bought a dress instead with coloured swirls on it and bell sleeves. I thought about a raised heel but the only shoes I have with any kind of high heel hurt my feet, I'm so used to wearing my Uggs, so I dug out some cowboy-style boots I bought years ago with virtually no heel. From the expression on Elen's face she's not impressed.

'Right. You are wearing two outfits at once. And those boots have to go.'

'Sorry?'

'Wait there.'

Where does she think I'm going to go?

She leaves the room and returns with something blue and a belt.

'Show me the top of your jeans.'

I lift the dress. The jeans are holding in my soft bit.

'I knew you had a good waist! Why do you always hide it? Take the dress off.'

'Eh?'

'Take it off. I've seen girls in their bras before, Alice.'

I pull it over my head and hand it to her. She nods and hands me the blue top. I'm horribly conscious of my big bazookas slightly spilling over my bra. I really need to buy some better-fitting underwear. She doesn't seem to notice as she examines my purchase.

'This is a nice dress, actually. It'll look great with a big belt for work. But it's not for going out. Tonight you should wear that top. Go on, put it on.'

It's made of soft material and when I put it on it falls near the hips and has three-quarter, batwing sleeves. Its neck is slashed so it falls off one shoulder and it drapes rather than clings. It has sparkly bits and is very '1980s', the one decade *no-one* should revisit. But I can't lie, I like it, even though it's electric blue. I feel like Olivia Newton John. She then hands me the thick leather belt with a huge buckle.

'Put it on. It's too baggy otherwise.'

I do as I'm told. She claps her hands then bounds over to the side of the room and grabs a pair of boots from under a telephone table.

'These are good. They've got a three-inch heel but it's a

block – look. Just as comfy as those flat things but a bit more funky. What size are you?'

'Five.'

'Bingo!'

She pours us another large Prosecco as I try them on. They're broken-down leather and stupidly comfy. I think they're a bit too cool for me but she drags me to a mirror. Her bedroom is painted an old-fashioned Victorian green and has a black wrought-iron bed and a grandmother clock. I am so jealous. She seems very pleased with the effect and I have to say, the high-waisted jeans and the belt have done a lot for my shape. I'm still perturbed that when I turn around you can see the fullness of my massive backside, but it is slightly balanced by the heel height.

'Wow, Alice. That's more like it.'

She hands me a wipe.

'Take off the lipstick though. And hold still.'

I applied some dark lipstick to go with the dress I was wearing. It was at the bottom of my cosmetic bag in the bathroom. I don't usually wear lipstick. I think about protesting then decide to allow myself to be her little project, just for tonight. She takes eyeliner from the make-up bag on the dressing table.

'Close your eyes.'

She applies the liner then hands me a rose-coloured tube of gloss. I put some on. It tastes of cherries. I look in the mirror. I now have smoky black kohl liner smudged around my eyes making me look like Siouxsie Sioux's tamer sister. I'm not sure about this at all.

'Elen, I'm too grow-up for this kind of make-up, surely?'

'Shut up! You're not eighty! Plus I've balanced it with natural, glossy lips. That's very 'in' I'll have you know – and it goes great with the hair and shows off your eyes, so fucking stop it and come and have another drink.'

She has made me look totally different from my usual self. I look like a more mature version of my teenage self, actually. I don't know if this is good or bad.

'Thank you Elen. I'll get these back to you.'

'I know you will!'

I'm surprised when I find the Prosecco all gone. Elen brings a bottle of wine from the fridge and pours as I sink back onto her chaise-longue.

'Don't get too comfortable. We're leaving in twenty minutes.'

'Oh, Elen, it's so nice here. Can't we just stay in?'

'Not on your nelly. You need to play. Let's not forget, you told Harry you'd 'rip his fucking throat out'! That in itself calls for a night out. Plus you've lost weight. In one week your face has gone all angular. I mean, come on, what's going on? And please don't tell me you've just been having a few rows with Tommi. You're always having rows with Tommi. You don't always drop pounds overnight and go psycho on our boss.'

I consider lying then change my mind. Elen's a lovely girl and I feel comfy. Sod it.

'All right. But whatever I say now has to stay within these walls.'

She cocks her head. 'Okay.'

'Tommi went to a party for someone's birthday at work on Monday and came back in the middle of the night. Turns out some horrendous, honking, six-foot blonde from the office was sucking his cock in her car.'

To my annoyance, my eyes well up again. Elen springs from her seat and grabs a handful of tissues from a holder with a

Spanish dancing girl painted on it.

'*Nooooo*. That's horrendous. I'm so sorry.'

I place the tissues under my eyes to catch the tears before they wreck my eyeliner.

'Don't be sorry. It was inevitable.'

'What do you mean?'

'He shagged a mate of ours before I had Barney.'

She looks scandalised.

'Alice. What a dick. He's not even that fit. Not as fit as you.'

I can't help a little giggle.

'Did you actually catch them at it?'

'No, thank Christ. But she messaged him about it next morning and I saw. She's either very stupid or extremely calculating.'

'The *bitch*. She obviously knows he's married?'

'Well yeah, but she's single so it's not up to her to behave, is it? It's up to him. She says they go for lunch in the pub together.'

Her eyes widen.

'You spoke to her?'

'I called her. She blamed me for being frigid and a cow to him. Said he needed understanding.'

'Ewwww. I hate her. Have you thrown him out?'

'For now I have. He's staying with our friends.'

'You are so brave, Alice. Ringing her and making him go. I'm in awe. What a fucking bitch she was to say that.'

I pause as it starts to sink in a little bit. The hugeness of it all.

'The worst bit is, Barney's starting to get suspicious now. I mean I can't just walk away from Tommi, can I? We have a child.'

'Why not? You can't stay with someone who does what he just did. I would leave a man for kissing someone else, never mind… You know.'

'Not so easy to say when you have a child together, Elen.'

'Do you even fancy him now?'

I take a huge gulp of my wine.

'Alice? Do you?'

'I don't know. When I found out about "it" I was upset and jealous. But not jealous that she'd touched him. Not sexually jealous. Is that weird? I was more jealous that I wasn't getting any attention and he was. I'm like the bloody Gobi desert down there.'

I point to my crotch and Elen collapses into giggles and spills wine down herself. This lightens the mood so much I join in. When all's said and done, the situation is preposterous.

'I'm sorry for laughing, Alice. But from where I'm standing you just don't fancy him anymore. He obviously can't find your love button.'

'My what? I don't think I have one. I think mine dropped off.'

Elen laughs.

'Maybe the desert wouldn't be so dry if you could water it from someone else's can, if you see what I mean?'

I raise an eyebrow.

'My friend Smithy said virtually the same thing.'

'Good for Smithy. Now, let's order a cab. There's someone who wants to water my desert tonight and he'll be arriving at The Dog any minute.'

CHAPTER EIGHT

The Dog is all wood and knackered green leather. There are music posters everywhere and several booths as well as tables and chairs and a dance floor. I am relieved that when Elen spots her friends – two lads with 1960s mop haircuts and variations of what looks like exactly the same outfit, plus a shy girl called Sam who barely looks up when I say hello – they have commandeered the booth furthest from the speakers so we can have some sort of conversation. Less joy comes from a quick scan of the clientele. All babies. I make a 'drink' sign to Elen who smiles and gives me the thumbs up and I wade through young bodies to the bar. It's only when I get there that I realise I didn't ask the others what they wanted. Sod it. The barman has a big afro and a sweet face. When he finally gets to me, I ask for a bottle of Prosecco on ice and he laughs. I glare at him and he straightens his expression.

'Sorry, but we don't have Prosecco. We have house white, house red, beer, cider and spirits. Oh and a few mixers. Our regulars don't usually want more than a bucket of our 'drink of the night' with a straw to suck it down with.'

I'm embarrassed and laugh to cover it up. What was I thinking, coming here? I'm way out of my depth. I must look so bloody ridiculous.

'Okay then. Give me a bottle of vodka, please. On ice if you can.'

'You do realise how expensive that will be?'

I pull out my emergency credit card.

'I don't give a shit. I just want to get very very drunk.'

He high fives me, chuckling. Suddenly I feel less stupid. Back at the table, the arrival of glasses, a bottle of vodka and a huge jug of iced cranberry juice, is greeted with a loud cheer and a look of slight confusion from Elen's friends, who evidently don't usually have a sugar-mummy with them on their nights out. Elen kisses me on the cheek as I sit, then slips back into flirtatious conversation with the young man who I think is called Noah. Noah, like the other boy, Gav, looks like he should be in an Indie rock band. An expensive one, though. He's all clean with perfectly layered hair and expensive-looking jeans. Gav is the same but with bleached white hair. He looks like a child, a child with tattoos. He could easily be fourteen but I suspect he isn't. I think he also likes Elen because he keeps making jokes and basically trying to break up the flirtation while Sam watches him quietly, eyes full of want.

I don't miss that kind of mess. That horrible feeling of fancying and not being fancied back. Not even being noticed. That's why I was so relieved when I met Ben, my first boyfriend, and why I clung on for so long to a young man who basically bored the hell out of me. And that's also why I was so happy when I met Tommi. All of the doubt was removed. We met in a bar, we laughed together and our relationship developed. We lived together in our first flat within a year and were solid pretty much immediately.

A holiday romance, six months before Tommi, was the only

'risky' relationship I ever allowed myself. It was quite plain I couldn't settle down with Gene, the surf instructor from Cape Town: I was only there for two weeks. But in that fortnight I felt more out of control with lust than I have ever felt before or since. Even in the newest days with Tommi, when we'd stay in a hotel in Blackpool and only leave the room to eat, it still wasn't that heady mix of sunshine, rampant freedom and danger of the unknown. Plus Gene was not my 'type' then. He was a grown man, covered in knackered tattoos and with a wealth of experience, that I couldn't begin to understand. I was naive and he was worldly wise. How many times since have I wished that I'd kept in contact with Gene? Just to have that link with a carefree world that is now cut off from me.

I snap out of my thoughts, vodka in hand, as another 'boy' joins us, dropping into the seat opposite and clasping hands with Noah in greeting. He is not so clean cut or young-looking as the others. I reckon he's about twenty-six. He has thick dreaded hair, dark dusky skin, and the most beautiful almond-shaped eyes with black irises. He's wearing a grey shirt and a maroon waistcoat with black canvas trousers. He reminds me of someone... Who? Jim Morrison. He looks like Jim Morrison. If Jim Morrison had brown skin and a raised scar across his cheek. I hope that's an innocent scar and not some horrible knife thing. I am such a mum. As he's discussing some problem with a mic stand with Noah, Elen pipes up.

'Alice, this is Noah's mate Philo. Philo, this is Alice, my friend from work.'

'Hello...!'

I proffer my hand, already woozy from fizz, wine and vodka, and he takes it and nods.

'Hey Alice. Nice to meet you.'

When he looks at me I want to look away. He has a very intense gaze and he's too handsome to focus on. I'm scared that I'll stare, probably at that scar, and make a fool of myself. Horribly, I think my cheeks have gone red. I'll bet his mother has had a nightmare with him; I can't imagine a young lady in this bar who would be able to resist him. Not knowing what else to do, I push a glass towards him.

'You want some vodka?'

'Sweet!'

He smiles and the room seems to brighten. There's a slight gap between his front teeth and a glint in his eye. I knew it. Naughty and he knows it. I look down at the table again. I am nearly forty, I am nearly forty, I am nearly forty. I repeat this to myself, swallowing another mouthful of alcoholic cranberry. Usually when I feel this (passing) attraction, I stop it dead in its tracks, knowing that, no matter how gorgeous, I'm not allowed to do any more than look. Today I'm adrift. Today I'm not even living in the same house as Tommi (for now). I'm having my first proper night out in I don't know how long and my son and partner are a hundred and fifty miles away. That thought makes me feel afraid and sad and just the teeniest bit high.

And that's when Stevie Marriot saves me. To my utter surprise and joy I hear the opening chords to 'Tin Soldier' by the Small Faces. I can't believe they play this old stuff here. Even I'm too young for this music. My head whips up and without a thought I beam at the whole table.

'I'm going to *dance*!'

The floor isn't packed but there are enough people for me not to feel ridiculous. Anyway, the drink has helped enormously and it just feels fantastic to be moving to a beat among a bunch of warm bodies, with music blocking my thoughts. I even know the words, which I sing with abandon. A girl dancing next to me notices and sings them right back at me with a big smile on her face. Then I feel a hand on my waist and I see that Elen and Philo have joined me. Elen, like me, is from the 'shake your arse and wave your hands' school of dancing. For a second we hug, then carry on. I think she's pissed. Philo, I notice, is totally unself-conscious on the dance floor. He undulates, almost like a snake, and I see more than one pair of eyes appraising him as he moves. Now that I can snatch glances at him without seeming creepy, I can fully take in his perfection. Nothing about him has softened or sagged or expanded. He is from a world where your whole life is ahead of you and you can do absolutely anything and everything. It shows in the openness of his face, the unself-conscious way he moves and the way he can probably throw on anything he finds in a drawer and still look good. No bloated waistline or cynical sneer or tired pouches. As the song changes to another old classic, I decide I just want to dance and dance. Elen goes back for round two of 'Noah-time' but I stay and so, to my surprise, does Philo.

Four, five, six songs later and I'm still on the dance floor. Philo disappears once for about thirty seconds and returns with our drinks, freshly filled, which we sip as we strut to The Kinks. Suddenly, the stress of the whole week is temporarily shoved into a wardrobe at the back of my mind. Now it's just music and dancing and fun. Things I have been missing terribly. All at once I think of my little boy, who I said good night to via Tommi just before I came here. Tommi was surprised I was at Elen's; I told him we were sharing wine and chatting. He didn't need to know I was going out. Barney said his nana had given him a mix-up of sweets and a new toy car. It occurs to me he's probably still up, bouncing off the walls, as I'm dancing. Half of me wants to cry when I think this but the drunk half, knowing he's safe and with family, feels free to have a good time. For the first time in an age – my time.

As the next song finishes, Philo takes a box of fags from his breast pocket and nods his head towards the exit. Dizzy and flushed, I follow him. Outside, the air is as crisp as an apple and I'm glad of the chill as it helps clear the fuzziness in my head. To be honest, I'm not half as sozzled as I should be, as the exercise has sobered me up. The rush I feel from dancing must be akin to the rush other people get from drugs. I've never had any interest in narcotics. Everything I've tried but weed has made me loopy and upset, but if others get a buzz from drugs like I do from music, then I understand. Philo leads me to a locked doorway around the corner that acts as a little shelter from the breeze, and offers me the battered packet.

'God, I've not had a cigarette in ten years. Can I maybe just have a toot on yours?'

'Of course you can, if you really want to break a ten-year rule.'

I shiver a little. He lights up. His close proximity is not lost on me.

'So how come I've not met you before?'

He has a soft voice with a London accent. I shrug.

'I don't usually come out. I have a little boy and, erm... a partner. Sort of.'

Did I just say 'sort of'? His face becomes one big, cheeky smile.

'So you're a MILF!'

CHAPTER EIGHT

My laugh is a bark that turns into a cough. This makes him choke on his cigarette. Oh God, I'm giggling.

'Don't say that! 'MILF' marks you out, doesn't it? You're not attractive for yourself any more. You're attractive despite having pushed out a child. Like the fact you're not a pendulous, fat-uddered cow with a face like a broken bassoon earns you some kind of sympathy vote.'

'Talk about over-thinking. It simply means you're a woman who has a child and you're um... very attractive.'

He glances at me then takes a drag.

'Anyway, what do you mean, you have a partner "sort of"?'

'I shouldn't have said that. I have a partner totally.'

'But?'

'But?'

'Oh, come on. There's a "but" screaming out of you. There is totally a "but"...'

'He. Actually, I don't want to talk about it and spoil the night.'

'That bad? He cheated?'

'Kind of.'

'Kind of?'

'Pretty much.'

'What a twat.'

He smiles that ridiculous light-bulb-going-on-in-a-cave smile. I shouldn't be smiling back.

'Well, you know what that means, don't you?'

'I'm sure you're going to tell me.'

I take the proffered cigarette and struggle not to cough my guts up after one tiny draw.

'You can't let him off. You've got to even things up.'

'Why do people keep saying that?'

A couple of rangy boys in hoodies several feet away, no doubt smoking Woodbines, turn in surprise at my sudden loudness. I wave an apology. They look away again.

Philo laughs. 'Because it's true.'

For a second he looks almost shy, then he takes a drag and cranks up his lightbulb smile.

'If you're looking for volunteers...'

Just then Elen appears, Elen who doesn't smoke. She looks tipsy and worried. Her face softens with relief when she sees us.

'Where have you been? I came to dance and you'd gone.'

'I was just having a chat with Philo. While he smokes his cigarette. Filthy habit by the way, Philo.'

He winks. Elen doesn't laugh.

'Philo, you'd better not be trying to get into my friend's knickers. I know what you're like.'

She's slurring, bless her. He does his best to look wounded.

'Elen, I'm having a nice chat with Alice. Why do you have to lower the tone?'

Drunken confusion crosses her face.

'Oh. Sorry. Alice, sorry, it's just he never stays with anyone more than five minutes and...'

I put my hand on her arm.

'Elen, that's very sweet but I'm a big girl. We were just having a laugh, weren't we, Philo?'

'Yup.'

She gives me a hug and whispers in my ear.

'Are you really having fun?'

'Yes, totally. Thanks to you.'

She smiles and looks tearful at the same time, then wanders shakily back into the pub.

CHAPTER EIGHT

'Wow. Methinks Elen is rather drunk. And she seems to have the idea you're a bad boy.'

He finishes his cigarette and shoots me another glance.

'She has no idea how bad I am.'

To my own ears, my laugh sounds like a distress cry.

CHAPTER NINE

We dance for another hour. Maybe more, I don't even know. But I do know I'm now ready to go home. Elen departed in a drunken mess about half an hour ago with Noah by her side. A crestfallen Gav was left with a clearly delighted Sam, who seems now to be talking a lot more, while stroking his leg. I sit down with a half pint of tap water in front of me and wonder just how sweaty and foul I'll look when the house lights go up. With Elen gone I'm a little less confident than before, plus I'm feeling pretty sober now. I decide to scarper before my face comes under scrutiny and quickly grab my teensy bag and stand. In a trice Philo, who'd been at the loos, is by my side.

'You want me to take you to a cheap taxi place? It's on my way home.'

I can't really say no, can I? Funnily enough, I don't want to leave with him. Even though we've had a brilliant night, it would be too clichéd to cop off with someone right now just to score a brownie point against Tommi. Because that's what I'd be doing, right? Snogging to redress the balance. And actually, more importantly, I'm scared. I've been off the market for years. I doubt I'd know what to do.

CHAPTER NINE

As we wander down the road, which is lined with young people eating street food and sitting in shop doorways, vomiting, arguing and chatting, I'm struck by this other world that I haven't been part of for such a long time. I don't miss it exactly. I just miss the possibilities of my twenties. The very aimlessness that I never really experienced. Why did I need to settle down so young? Was it because my parents met young? When Philo takes my hand, I almost pull it away but then don't. It feels warm as he leads me past bars and emptying late-night restaurants and neon signs for closed up shops that sell belly rings and PVC trousers. I love looking at the lights, I could be anywhere in the world right now. Suddenly we take a right down a side street and I see a taxi sign up ahead, with men standing by it, chatting in a language I don't recognise. Just before we reach it, Philo swings me round, almost dances me, into an archway with a door which has a big metal three on it. He pulls a key out of his back pocket.

'What's happening?'

'You're coming in for a drink before you get your taxi.'

'In where?'

He smiles. Neon glints off his teeth.

'My place of course... Please?'

Of course I'm not going to.

'One drink.'

Oops. I didn't mean to say that.

He squeezes my hand tighter before letting go. The door opens with a creak and we ascend three flights of darkened stairs. As he opens his door on the top flight, he flicks on a light and lets me go in first.

'Don't worry about tip-toeing, the two guys downstairs work nights. I promised them I wouldn't play loud music by day and they don't make a noise when they get in from work.'

'That's nice of them.'

'Most people are nice if you're friendly.'

We pass through his tiny hallway and into the living room. It's gloomy and for a moment I experience a surge of panic. I'm out of my depth here and I don't know why I've accompanied this stranger into his flat. But he quickly lights candles, of which he has many, and a small lamp with an orange bulb in it. He has a big couch, a small wingback chair which looks like it might be red, but I can't properly tell in the flickering light, and lots of CDs and books on shelves lining the walls. On the floor he has a lot of musical equipment and he has a guitar on a stand next to the stereo and small TV. The candles are scented so it smells lovely. Fruit and cinnamon. I marvel that a young man would think of such a thing. It's quite clean in here too. I'm impressed and forget my misgivings as I look around me while perched on the sofa, which has seen better days but is very large and comfy.

'Right. There's beer and there are three cans of gin and tonic that my mate left the other night.'

I suspect the gins are a girl's, as young men rarely drink such things. But that's none of my business.

'Could I just have a glass of water, please? I'm feeling nice and mellow, I don't want to tip over into feeling sick.'

'Of course.'

He gets a beer for himself and a water for me, and joins me on the sofa. He picks up a remote and presses a button. Suddenly there's music.

'I usually fall asleep to this. It's my chill-out mix.'

After a night of crazy dancing it should be perfect. It is

CHAPTER NINE

perfect. But I can't help feeling self-conscious. No matter how much I'm angry with Tommi, I am committing a crime against my relationship, surely, just by being here? I take a sip of water and Philo drinks his beer. He's regarding me with those intense eyes again and it strikes me how absurd it is that I should be in this sweet-smelling flat with this beautiful young man who's entering the prime of his life, a musician no less, when I've already exited my prime and am hurtling towards the place of no return with a partner and son in tow. Why does he even want me here?

'What's wrong?'

'Sorry?'

'You looked so sad suddenly.'

'Did I?'

'Still beautiful though. What were you thinking about? Home?'

I haven't been called beautiful in a long time. Is that how young people pull these days?

'No. I was just thinking of how life whizzes past. I was your age five minutes ago.'

He shouldn't be looking at me with such concern. I smile to make him happy again. He takes my glass away and puts it on the floor. He doesn't say anything else. Just reaches forward and places his mouth on mine. I can feel a tremor in his lips. Not as confident as he pretends then? Or is it because I seem a woman of experience to him? My belly lurches but he is so gentle that I don't resist. My eyes close as his mouth opens and I glory in the fullness of his lips, the warmth of his beer and smoke saliva, the way his tongue unapologetically enters my mouth. Feeling his tongue probing and tasting its way around mine causes a stab of heat. I feel ripples of it spreading through me and find myself suddenly placing both hands at the back of his neck and pulling him violently to me. My enthusiasm surprises me. God, he's actually delicious. I'm sucking on his mouth and I want to suck the rest of him in, eat him alive. The fact I shouldn't be here and I'm supposed to be 'responsible' is suddenly unimportant.

I stop and pull back. His brow furrows.

'Are you okay?'

He licks the moisture from his lips. I want to do it for him. I'm scared of being this turned on.

'I don't know. Can I just grab one of those gins?'

He jumps out of the seat and returns with a can. He pops the ring pull and hands it to me, sitting once more with his leg pressed against mine. My heart is beating out of my chest. I take a swig or two then put it down. The cool liquid calms me and I reach to touch the raised-up scar on his face. An imperfection that enhances the whole.

'What happened?'

'A psychopath's girlfriend came on to me in a club. I didn't know she was with someone. He tried to kill me.'

'You're kidding. With a knife?'

'Nope. Bottle. He was drunk; lucky I pulled back so he only cut me once or I'd have a face like lumpy porridge.'

'Christ.'

'As it stands it gives me a nice bad-boy image!'

I am in a quandary. Stop this right now or steal another snog then run for it?

Boldly I lean and kiss his scar. He lets me, then turns his face so my lips are on his again. This time he caresses my back as my hands snake around his lithe waist. I can't believe how smooth his skin is under his shirt, or the way I seem to be

CHAPTER NINE

liquefying as he kisses me. As I sink against the back of the sofa his hand begins to move down my collarbone. I know what's coming next and I should resist but I don't. Extraordinarily, as he leisurely makes his way down, inching his fingers inside Elen's blue top, caressing my skin, I find myself wanting to scream at him to hurry up. But instead I kiss him like I'm drowning and when, finally, his palm comes to rest on my bra, the bra I didn't expect to be under scrutiny tonight, a black boring thing that's too fucking small, I let out a gasp and thrust my chest into his hand.

Responding in kind, he rips the cup out of the way and takes my nipple between his fingers, forcing a cry from me, then a small yelp as he yanks the other cup out of the way.

Awkwardly we manoeuvre ourselves so that I am on my back. The strangeness of this situation is now making me feel like I'm an inexperienced teenager having her first sexual encounter. Helpless but at the same time hungry. As I lie there I watch in wonder as he pulls his waistcoat and shirt straight over his head to reveal his beautiful, dark-skinned, almost hairless torso, with a belly of sinew and flat planes and a silver dolphin hanging round his neck on a long black thong. I never expected to see a man, a man who isn't Tommi, a gorgeous man-boy in fact, take his clothes off in front of me. And certainly not with such look of anticipation on his face.

The settee is so wide that he can lie beside me, and now, as he kisses my face and neck, he unbuckles Elen's large belt, fumbling for a moment or two until I help him. All at once it's on the floor and he's raising my top until he's exposed my bra and breasts. With one more bite to my bottom lip he mounts me, straddling my hips, then bends his face to a nipple, while taking the other breast in his hand. My sharp intake of breath spurs him on as he moves his nose against the pink bud, then kisses and licks all the way around it before finally taking it in his mouth. I don't know if he's a master of sexual teasing or he is just hitting lucky, but the way he's messing with me sends me through the roof. When my nipple is thoroughly wet and the energy is pinging around my body like a pin-ball, he moves to the other one and does the same.

God, oh God. Should I stop him? I so want more. This might be the only chance I get to experience the sheer abandoned energy of a very young man.

But I can't do it.

There's something about him actually inserting himself into me that would be too far too personal, too much of a betrayal to my relationship. I can hear a prim voice inside, telling me to stop what I'm doing and go home. I've heard it so many times in my life. Telling me to be cautious, warning me of consequences. But even though it's probably right, the rebel in me isn't quite ready to stop yet.

I rub my hands over his smooth chest before dipping my head and suddenly biting one brown nipple. He groans, so I do it to the other one. Then, with a little bit of rearranging, he manages to get his hands to the front of my jeans and unfasten the top button. I hold my breath. As the second and third button pop, I find myself panting with anticipation and before he can get my zip fully down, I suddenly thrust into his waistband and grip his cock. It is hot and hard and seems surprisingly ample for such a slight man-boy. I feel him freeze as I stroke him, then I hear him suck air through his teeth. For a while he remains completely still, apart from one rogue hand that stealthily lowers my zip and insinuates itself into my pants.

CHAPTER NINE

Like two fifteen-year-olds at a cider party we pleasure each other. I move against that devilish hand while I rub my thumb against the very tip of his cock, still inside his shorts, before rhythmically moving up and down the shaft. His gasps are loud and unashamed as I begin to arch into a finger which is sending constant beats of pleasure through me. I'm now pretty sure he's found that love button Elen mentioned as he begins to rub harder against me. *So it hasn't fallen off.* Then out of nowhere the whole world goes white in my head and I can hear nothing but my own cries as I climax against the fingertip of a boy I met about six hours ago.

As the wave hits then begins to subside, he surprises me by pushing in closer and continuing to rub and caress, whispering, 'Come again for me, let me hear you... Come on Alice, let me hear you come again.'

I don't know if it's the surprise that he keeps going, or hearing him use my name so forcefully at such an intimate moment, but it works and my whole body quivers as I come again. This has not happened to me for a long time. I am so shocked I begin to laugh. After a while, he smiles and kisses me softly, then shakes his head.

'Jesus. I haven't jizzed in my boxers since I was sixteen! You little minx.'

I flush with pleasure. I just made him come without actually, technically, having sex. And he's calling me a minx like I'm the teenager and he's the grown-up. God, that was good. And no body fluids were exchanged except saliva. That's one up on Tommi. Plus, he got Rabbit Face. Look who I pulled!

Philo sits up and gets out a fag. He is still in his open trousers. It occurs to me I felt his cock but didn't see it. His chest and belly and wiry arms are so perfect. Almost too perfect. Then

I notice the scars on his inner arm. About six cut marks. He sees me notice as I'm fixing my bra and pulling my top into place.

'Don't worry, they're five years old. I used to be a bit melodramatic.'

Five years old. Like Barney. Agghh. Don't think about him now, for Christ's sake.

Of course, I immediately worry. The other side to being young: everything is so emotional and important.

'You tried to kill yourself?'

He holds out his arm for closer inspection.

'Look. Not deep. Superficial, in fact. I got mad at my mother, got drunk and carved my arm up a bit with a penknife. It can't have been that bad, I fell asleep bleeding and woke up with scabs. Not dead.'

'You wouldn't do that now, would you?'

'Of course not. I like messing about with MILFs too much.'

I slap his hand and he laughs. He picks up his beer and I retrieve my gin. Then he leans forward to kiss me.

'You've got great tits.'

'*What?*'

'Sorry. But I love big tits. Not fake ones, proper ones. It's like being in a Fellini film.'

'Great tits.' Not exactly poetry. But I thought no-one would ever find them sexy again. I thought Tommi was making do with these matronly orbs instead of my little perky C-cups; so right now, I'm embarrassingly complimented. Plus he knows who Federico Fellini is. He's a box of surprises this one.

'Can you stay tonight, Alice? I'd really really like you to.'

Jesus, he's ready for more. Part of me would love to stay and see what else this naughty boy can do. But I mustn't. Because if I do, I will have sex with him properly, and be guilt-stricken. And I can't let this young Adonis see my morning face and bed-hair. I would have to jump to my death from his window simply to avoid the humiliation.

I shake my head.

'Thank you. That is very tempting but I really have to get home. Stuff to do tomorrow and all that.'

'Damn! Look, I go to The Dog on Fridays quite a lot. Come back! Have another night out soon. Unless you want my number? Or I could take yours?'

'Erm - might be tricky. I'm a mummy. I can't be sexting young musicians and you probably have a queue of groupies; I have to behave.'

'Can't you be one of my groupies?'

'No. I don't even know if you're a good musician!'

He grabs up the guitar and begins to play. Of course, he's great. I didn't expect anything less. For a second I waver. But instead I put on my boots – Elen's boots. When I stand he gets up too but I hold up a hand.

'Don't come out, the taxi place is just outside the door.'

'Bossy.'

He steps forward and kisses me. Already I want to eat him again. Swallow him up. I am so tempted to stay for more. Instead I break away, give him one last peck and leave, last of the can of gin and tonic in my hand.

Outside, I suck in the cold air and lean against a wall.

I'm shocked at how much fun it is redressing the balance. My first (and perhaps only) deviation from my relationship with Tommi and I've cut it short. Idiot. I wonder if Tommi would cut it short, in my shoes. Right now I feel surprisingly guilt-free as far as Tommi's concerned. In fact, I'm sorely tempted to knock and go back in. Granted, I started off a little self-conscious and I held back, but it got better. Maybe it would be fun to go further?

Best jump into a cab, quick.

CHAPTER TEN

Smithy is a bit drunk. I texted him and he told me Suze was staying at her sister's. We've Skyped.

'So. How's it all going? Is he still chucked out?'

'Yes. Smithy, why are you so twatted?'

'I've just had a night to myself. And a curry. I'm enjoying myself. In case you haven't noticed, it's very late.'

'Okay. Well, yes, it is two o'clock in the morning.'

'What have you been up to until this late hour?'

'Nothing.'

'Actually, I don't have to ask. You've got that rosy glow.'

'Stop it!'

'Ha. Don't look so scared. I don't care what you've been doing. You certainly look happier than last time I spoke to you.'

'Do I?'

'Yes, you bloody do. And good on you.'

'I… erm… kissed somebody, Smithy.'

I can't tell him the full details, I really can't.

'You kissed somebody. Kissed somebody. So what? That doesn't even count.'

'Eh?'

'Jesus Al, that's nothing to worry about. In the grand scheme of dedicating years of your life to a relationship with someone, how can a cheeky kiss be a bad thing? Just to remind yourself you're alive?'

'Smithy! Have you..?'

He puts his hands over his mouth.

'Speak no evil, Alice. Speak no evil.'

'But…'

'Suze is my darlin'. She's my star. But she bloody hates… you know.'

'But…'

'She's got a lot on her plate. Bigger fish to fry…'

'Do you still love her, Smithy?'

'With all of my heart. With my lungs, Al. Just don't torture yourself over nothing..'.

'What if I'd gone further, Smithy?'

'Who bloody cares. So long as it made you feel better, you're a long time dead. That idiot of yours, he doesn't know what he's got…'

'I miss you, Smithy.'

'I miss you too. The real you. Not the one that's been battered into the ground. Do more kissing, it suits you.'

I love Smithy.

CHAPTER ELEVEN

I can hear Tommi's car approaching and I am aching for a cuddle from Barney. After my rollicking Friday night, Saturday (yesterday) became my first proper lie-in in years. And I certainly needed it. The drink, the dancing and the... yes... that. I thought I wouldn't sleep because of guilt but I fell straight into a coma after my Skype and only jolted awake at 11.00 a.m. when my mobile phone went off next to my head and scared the life out of me. It was Tommi calling so Barney could speak to me and he sounded mighty suspicious when he heard the just-woken-up rasp.

'Are you still in bed?'

'Yes, I'm not feeling well. I think I'm getting a cold.'

The lie came easily and I could sense his relief.

'Oh, sorry about that. Well, Barney has something to tell you.'

There was a fumbling at the other end then Barney's chirp had me grinning.

'Mummy, I played badminton and I beat Gramps twice!'

'Oh, well done, darling. Are you having a good time?'

'Brilliant. But I miss you. Why aren't you here?'

'I'm not feeling too well. And I'm working, too. But I'll see you tomorrow!'

'Okay.'

'Have a lovely barbecue.'

'I will. Gramps bought me a super-duper mega hot-dog. He says if I can eat it all he'll give me a medal. I'll save you a sausage.'

'Tell Nana, happy birthday from me.'

'Yeah. Love you.'

'Love ya.'

Barney had already gone. Tommi was back.

'I love you too, Alice. It's not the same here without you.'

'Sorry Tommi, but you know…'

'I know, I know. But I really want to sort things out soon. I want to come home.'

'Don't say anything now, please. Your mum might hear. It'll spoil her birthday.'

'Of course, that's why I'm hiding in a bush.'

I couldn't help laughing. The fool.

'You're hiding in a bush, are you?'

'I've pulled a branch off and I'm holding it over my head so I'll blend in. They'll never know I'm here.'

'Check outside your bush, they're probably all crowded round listening.'

Suddenly he whispered.

'I think you're right. I can see their feet. Let's speak later.'

Making me laugh was always Tommi's biggest talent. And once more he'd succeeded. But I was glad not to be at his mother's this weekend. Much as I love his parents, I would have said something snarky to their son and he would have had to admit what he'd been up to. Plus Friday night wouldn't have happened.

CHAPTER ELEVEN

Snuggled under my duvet, on the sofa with *Murder She Wrote*, a full cafétière and a couple of paracetamol on Saturday afternoon, I'd had the leisure and the space to think again about what had happened with Philo. I had committed a sin against my relationship. Suddenly Tommi's actions were more understandable than I'd acknowledged before. Being fancied is fantastic. Tommi and I had fallen into a routine. One that had been driving me nuts. And now we'd both done something to break it. What did that mean for us?

Try as I might to think about my relationship, my thoughts kept straying back to Philo. To his lips, how he tasted, how his skin smelled and how tantalising it was to be touched by new hands, kissed by a new mouth. As I thought about us kissing and what he did to me I felt a mixture of the horrible shame that had been lacking the night before and a flush of something akin to breathless ardour. I had to try very hard not to imagine what it would be like do it again and eventually I'd had to pleasure myself simply to refocus my mind. Masturbation has never been my thing so the force of the orgasm caused by my own fingers was a whole new surprise in itself.

I spent most of the rest of the day dozing, daydreaming and drinking water and found it difficult to sleep at night without Barney in the house, so put on some music and read a while.

This morning, I went to a lovely coffee house up the road and had an almond croissant and a giant cappuccino while reading a book I bought almost a year ago but hadn't had time to open yet. Again, it was bliss. But now, the sound of a car containing my boy is a wonderful thing. This is one of the dichotomies of motherhood; sometimes being a mum is just too much, but more than a night away and you start missing your child terribly.

Tommi uses his key to enter and Barney streaks straight through to the living room.

'MUMMMMMMMY!'

He finds me and wraps me in a titanic, spindly-armed bear-hug. I grab him back and we roll around the floor, laughing. Tommi follows him in. He is wearing jeans and a smart sweater, with tousled hair. His hair goes mad when he washes it – it takes a day or two to flatten down. Today he looks like Shaggy from *Scooby Do* so he must have had a shower at his mum's. He is his usual handsome self but his eyes look tired. When he sits, there's a small gasp of exertion. He's not used to having Barney without me, and this was at his parents' house. Imagine if it had just been the two of them for the weekend. He'd probably be in tears by now.

Barney also looks tired, a testament, no doubt, to staying up much too late with his cousins and eating too many e-numbers.

'Okay you. Some dinner and a bath, then I think you should watch a film in bed. You choose. We need to get you nice and rested for school.'

He doesn't even protest. Just squeezes me again and says, 'Can I watch something spooky?'

'Not too spooky or you'll wake up scared in the night. Funny spooky, okay?'

'Gramps let me watch *Dracula*!'

I look to Tommi who shrugs guiltily.

'The cousins and my dad snuggled on cushions, watching old movies and eating popcorn. What could I say?'

Nothing of course. I would have loved that when I was little.

'No wonder you look so tired! Now, I'm sure Daddy would like a glass of wine while you have a splash?'

CHAPTER ELEVEN

Barney smiles from me to his dad, obviously delighted that things seem 'better'. Tommi also looks happy when I hand him a globe of vino and offer him the remains of the hot chicken I bought this afternoon and the potatoes and veg that I cooked too much of. (Out of habit I suppose.) He happily settles down at the kitchen table as I run Barney a bath and find him some pyjamas. After forty-five minutes Barney is tucked up, as instructed, already looking heavy-eyed after a bowl of pasta, a wash and a giant hug. I don't predict him staying awake long enough to see much of the movie or have a story from me. But he's happy, so that's fine. He gives me another squeeze before I leave him.

'Mummy, you and Daddy are my favourites. We're all very happy, aren't we?'

Told you he was smart.

'Of course we are. And we love you very much, Barney Boo!'

I kiss his soft clean cheek then bury my nose in his washing-machine-fresh pyjama top. He giggles sleepily and I go downstairs to where his daddy is nodding off on the sofa, glass in hand, dinner finished. He looks up at me as I enter. I don't know if I see hope or wariness or maybe both in those grey eyes. I sink into the armchair and pull up my feet so I'm cross-legged.

'Nice hair. Very bold.'

I'd forgotten about my hair. I stroke a hand through it absently as I take a sip of my wine. I dried it with my big round brush today. It felt good as I walked along the street. Bouncy and light. Just like me.

'Thought I'd have a change.'

'You look well. Cold gone?'

'Eh? Oh, yeah, I slept it off. Not used to sleeping in!'

'Lucky you.'

'Lucky me? You usually sleep until at least ten on a Saturday morning while I make Barney's breakfast and take him to the park!'

'I know.'

He sounds sad. And more than a little afraid.

'I got drunk on Friday with Frank - '

Frank is Tommi's older brother. He's a bit self-pitying. He seems to think Tommi has all the breaks and that he, Frank, has been cursed by the gods. He hates his job as a civil servant, has unruly kids and he complains that his wife Amy just watches TV and goes to bed early. I think she's more depressed than he is, she just doesn't mention it as much.

'Did you tell him what's been going on here?'

He rubs his eyes, just like Barney does, a gesture that usually makes me want to hug him.

'God no, he'd love to think I'd fucked everything up. Mum, Dad and Frank think you've been helping out at work for the weekend. My mum says hi by the way – she loved the cardigan. Anyway, we just talked about the usual brotherly stuff and I eventually got to bed at one o'clock in the morning and then Barney jumped on me at half past six and the cousins joined him ten minutes later. I gave them some Rice Krispies, then Mum got up and I went back to bed, but I couldn't sleep because of the noise and I thought of you and how you always get up with Barney and I felt bad. I know I work all of the time and I'm tired, but you work too.'

'Yes, I do.'

'Like I said, I'll do my best to help while you sort out your work stuff.'

'Good. Harry's tearing his hair out.'

CHAPTER ELEVEN

'Why you want to put yourself out to help that idiot, I don't know.'

'Because I need my job. Now more than ever.'

He stares at me.

'Why now more than ever?'

'Because when something like this happens, Tommi, you suddenly don't know if anything in the world is secure anymore. Having my job makes me feel less wobbly.'

'I haven't been having an affair, Alice. You know that, don't you?'

'You've been having lunch together every day at the pub for God knows how long though, haven't you?'

His mouth drops open.

'The whole team have their lunch in the pub every day. Have you got a P.I. onto me?'

'Didn't need to. Apparently I'm a frigid cow who drove you into her arms and you just *love* your chats in the pub every day. It's the only thing that keeps you going. Her words, not mine, the morning I found the text. She really is a charmer.'

He has burning red spots, one on each cheek.

'You called her?'

'Of course I did. I was rather pissed off with you both. She informed me I was a shit partner to you, then slammed the phone down. Are you guys some kind of item at work?'

He opens then closes his mouth, reminding me of a guppy my granddad once had.

'No... We're just friends.'

'What, with benefits?'

If I hadn't had such a good night on Friday I would now be hissing like an alley cat. But in many ways I don't feel I have a leg to stand on. Not that I'm telling him that.

'No. As I said she's always been very friendly. I thought she might like me a bit, but it turns out she likes me a lot.'

'If I take too long getting my head round this, are you going to finish what you started with her? She sounds very keen.'

'Fuck, Alice, you almost sound like you want me to.'

'I don't know what I want. I've been really unhappy for a long time.'

'I noticed.'

'Please Tommi. I'm well aware I've been down and sometimes I've been horrible to you and I know it's not attractive. But still... I'm trying to work out if it's been me making myself unhappy, or me not enjoying being a domestic animal.'

'If you didn't want to be domestic, why did you keep asking me to move in with you within months of meeting me all those years ago?'

So far this has been an okay chat. I don't want to wake Barney with an argument. I lower my tone.

'There has got to be more to life than constant routine.'

'You're the one who never wants to go out because you're "too fat" and who never hangs out with my work mates because "they're boring" and who screams blue murder if someone gets crumbs on the rug. You've made yourself into a "domestic animal". Don't blame me.'

I'm starting to feel agitated now.

'So who would cook the dinners and get up with Barney and clean the house and be home by six if I didn't do it?'

'I would, or my mum would or your mum or whoever would. No-one has ever had to find out because you're always there controlling everything.'

'So that's all I am then? The gaoler?'

'Christ. No. You're still gorgeous, Alice. And when you're on

CHAPTER ELEVEN

form, you're a laugh and you're clever and life's good. But you talk to me like I'm younger than Barney half of the time and you're always wound up and when we have sex, it's actually just me having sex. I have no idea where you are. I mean, do you actually come on the rare occasions that we shag?'

I don't know what to say to this.

'I try, Tommi. But I've been so unhappy with how I look and so stressed about money. Plus there's always the chance of Barney running in. It's not exactly a sexy scenario, is it? Maybe this little rest will help me sort everything out in my head.'

'I don't want to stay over there forever, Alice. I can hear their kids running about all of the time instead of Barney. It's torture. Talia keeps patting my hand and asking if I need to talk. I don't want to talk to her. I want to talk to you.'

'So how come you confided that our sex life was shit to Emma, if you don't want to talk about us to other people?'

He looks freaked out. There's something I'm missing here. I'm sure of it. A piece of the puzzle I don't have. Or, possibly, I'm paranoid and insecure.

'I don't know why she said that to you.'

'Because she's infatuated? I mean, a colleague! How can I trust you working there, now? Every time you go to work I'll be wondering.'

'Alice. We just need to get on track again. Then you'll trust that I don't want anyone else. It was a mistake. I just wish you'd let me come back so we can start sorting things out here, in our own house.'

He puts down his glass and stands. I think he might be leaving but he walks to the armchair, and slightly lifts me so that he can sit down, with me perching unwillingly on his lap. He folds his arms around me and the familiar musk envelops me. He always smells nice. He kisses my cheek then, emboldened by me not pulling away, he kisses my mouth. Those lips I know so well with the downy hair above and below, so soft that he hardly has to shave. He feels comfortable and warm and, strangely, I am turned on by his proximity. More so than I have been in a long time. But as his mouth opens I stop him and turn the embrace into a hug. I am aroused because I had some naughtiness two nights ago and I want more. I am turned on by the thought of more caresses. Selfishly, I want to be fucked. But these caresses are from someone who will see the sex as a green light to moving back in. To things 'going back to how they were', to me forgetting the thrill of kissing a new young man with a scar on his cheek and a body of brown granite and satin.

I can't go there yet. I cannot be the woman I was before I saw that text from 'Em'. I need more time.

'Tommi, I'm sorry but I really need to go to bed. I have such a long week ahead of me.'

He smiles shyly. Or an approximation of shyness anyway.

'Can't I come with you?'

'Tommi…'

He stands. He doesn't look pleased.

I kiss his cheek and we hug again.

Then he leaves.

CHAPTER TWELVE

When I hand the carrier bag back to Elen with her boots, top and belt, she smiles like a giant cheese.

'Good night, wasn't it?'

'Certainly was. Got my freak on! - Is that what you young 'uns say? I noticed you disappeared with Noah, young lady. I hope he didn't take advantage. You were rather tipsy.'

'Oh, he was lovely. We both collapsed in a heap when we got to mine. Saturday morning was a different story though...'

I put my hands over my ears.

'I don't want to hear, you lucky git'.

'He is handsome, isn't he? And what about Philo. He was a bit keen. He usually spreads himself all over when we're out. He loves the ladies. But Friday he was stuck to you like super-glue.'

I try not to show anything on my face.

'I can't help it if I'm irresistible, can I? Shame he isn't ten years older.'

'Yeah. But still. Nice to be fancied.'

'Course'.

She doesn't know. Phew.

I look through my workload and start making calculations in

my head. An extra two hours tonight and Wednesday should be enough to finish my own stuff. Thursday and an extra couple of hours on Friday might be enough for Hassan's work, which to be fair he was half way through anyway. Plus I can do some of this from home. I can call the client, fax through what Hass's already done, (it's some chi-chi place in Mayfair and Harry is desperate not to lose the contract) check that they like it so far, then complete it myself. That will leave next week for any other jobs that aren't emergencies.

When I poke my head round Harry's door. He's on the phone. I catch the end of a conversation.

'Look. I'm sorry. I said I'm sorry. I'm always sorry. I've got to go now. Really. Please Melissa, I have to go. There's so much to do here.'

Melissa is his wife's name. He puts down the phone and puts his head in his hands. I duck back out and tap on the door this time. When I enter he is sitting up in his seat but still looks upset. I explain my plan and he seems a little happier but still distracted.

'Harry, are you all right?'

This is probably the nicest I have ever been to him. He gulps then nods as authoritatively as he can, but his baby-blues say it all.

'Yes, thank you, Alice. I'm fine. What about you? Someone was saying there might be, erm, a little awkwardness at home for you right now?'

'Really? Would that someone have a mouth the size of the Thames Estuary by any chance? And eyeshadow that alarms small mammals?'

Without warning, a pair of dimples appear in his cheeks.

'I'm afraid that's classified information. But suffice to say,

CHAPTER TWELVE

she alarms larger mammals too.'

'Well, let me tell you, Mr Percival, awkwardness at home or not, my brain is firing on all cylinders and for the first time in years I do not have to rush home every night. And incidentally, if I ever come in here wearing electric-blue eyeliner, shoot me in the head. Immediately.'

'Noted.'

'Good. Now, I think we've got some work to do.'

And work I do. At one o'clock I'm thinking of working through my lunch break, until I remember dropping Barney at school this morning. A Barney who was not pleased to find his father gone from the house again and who therefore played up all the way to his classroom, then hugged me piteously hard and begged me not to leave. While disentangling myself, I got many compliments from the mums on my new hair. And I finally woke up to the reality of my 'mummy uniform'. Looking around I saw tasteful greys, billowy kaftans and one or two try-hards in too much make-up and skyscraper heels. I decided I didn't want to look like any of them. I want to look like me. Whatever that is. I am sick of muted colours and baggy shapes. I am sick of looking as though I'm hiding something. If I want to change things I have to brave the high street again. And seeing as work is so close to the shops, lunchtime is as good as any to start.

So off I trot to the biggest, cheapest, high-street store in town, with the most ridiculous queues, and in twenty-five minutes I have piled into my basket several colourful dresses, more tight jeans, some pretty, fitted shirts, two thick belts, one black and one purple, an eyeliner and some gloss, tights, little tops and some faux-vintage jewellery going for a song. I also throw a pair of boots in there, similar to the ones that I borrowed from Elen, on sale for the princely sum of twenty pounds, a pencil skirt, a big, brown fake leather bag and three bras in the right cup size. (I hope. I measured myself after my shower on Sunday and if I'm not wrong I've been buying 34DD instead of 32F. I can't believe I'm an F!) I don't try anything on, though judging from my old clothes I seem to have gone down a dress size in a week. Every cloud and all that. I just run frantically round chucking whatever I want into my basket, like Supermarket Sweep, then wait ten minutes to get to the front of the queue to pay.

With fifteen minutes to spare I grab myself a tuna and sweetcorn sandwich and then, by chance, spot a pair of cherry-red court shoes with a buckle, a slight platform at the front and a thick, pretty heel at the back, in the shoe shop four doors from work. I can't resist trying them on. They're funky as hell and more comfortable than I thought raised shoes could ever be. Once again the emergency credit card comes out, building up an impressive tally by now, and I get back to work several minutes late and with three loaded bags. I don't have time to try any clothes until I get home but the Uggs, which are covered in scuff marks and are developing holes, are replaced by the cherry shoes, which feel surprisingly light and cool on my feet.

They're not as comfy to walk in as roomy, flat boots but they make me feel taller. As I work at the desk I find myself crossing and uncrossing my ankles. Elen is extremely impressed with the colour and I'm just praying the pencil skirt fits, as I reckon it'll be a killer combo. I laugh at myself for this sudden interest in clothes and then get my head back down to work. An hour later, as I get up to go to the little kitchen and put more coffee on (my second favourite liquid in the world) I find my shoes in the glare of the harpy's green eyeliner (she changes the colour sometimes just to keep us on our toes).

'Oh, someone's been pushing the boat out. Trying to spice it up for your fella then, are you?'

I'm not sure whether she's evil or just plain dumb. So without breaking my stride I smile.

'No, Belle, we already shag every day. If I spiced it up any more my poor fella would die of exhaustion.'

I hear several snickers, the loudest one from Elen and I could swear I even detect a snort from Harry's office. I return to my desk, grinning at Elen as she whispers, 'Buggy, you're outrageous.'

Then I notice a text message on my phone. I don't recognise the number:

Tommi came to see me last night, Alice. I told you he needed someone who understands him. When are you going to realise he's found his soulmate? Em

That certainly wipes the smile from my face. I suddenly feel a pounding in my temple. This woman is nuts. But did Tommi go round there after I turned him down? Maybe that's what happens when he doesn't get what he wants. And how did she get my number anyway, unless it was from his phone?

This is not good.

CHAPTER THIRTEEN

I keep my chat with Tommi brief. I call him at five o'clock, knowing he'll be leaving work soon to look after Barney.

'Did you go to see Emma last night?'

'What?'

'Emma. The one that nothing happened with?'

'Alice…'

'Alice, my arse. She texted me. I have no idea why she has my number but she's obviously nuts and you're encouraging her. Did you go and see her?'

There's a pause on the line.

'I'll take that as a yes then, shall I?'

'I promised I'd speak to her away from work. I owed her that much.'

'You owed her?'

'Yes. Al, it's complicated.'

'Don't Al me. It's complicated because you've made it complicated. I have no idea what's going on here but you tell her to stop contacting me and don't bother giving me any more guff about that night being a one-off. I am going to come home tonight after work and you are going to leave straight away, okay? Don't try to make me talk to you. Whatever you're

CHAPTER THIRTEEN

doing with her you're an imbecile for letting her rub my nose in it. I won't stand for it. Are you fucking her, Tommi?'

'No, of course not! I'm sorry she texted you. She's just young and hurt, I guess.'

'I don't care how old she is and don't bother being sorry. Just tell her to stop it.'

I put down the phone. My breathing is ragged. I wish I could throw something. Preferably at Tommi and that mental fucker he's messing with. What is he playing at? Elen looks concerned.

'Do you want me to stay late and help you, Buggy? Is everything okay?'

'Everything is fine, Elen, I just happen to be feeling a bit violent.'

'What's happened now?'

'Nothing. I just really need a glass of vino.'

'You up for Friday again? We can have a blow-out!'

I pause for a second. If I show up on Friday and Philo is there, I'll just come across like any other love-struck girl he messes with. And I'm not love-struck. Frankly, right now, I can do without blokes altogether.

'I think I'll probably still be working. But thanks anyway. And don't worry about staying tonight. I know what I'm doing, I just have to get on with it.'

'Okay.'

Work is a good distraction. The cleaners hoover around me at half past six and at seven, after popping his head out several times, Harry emerges from his office with two glasses and a nice looking bottle of white. He hands a glass to me. Bloody hell.

'How's it going?'

Bloody hell again.

'I've got quite a bit done actually. I have to be home by about eight-thirty, but I think I've done as much as I can today. Actually, I'm shattered. How about you?'

He pours.

'Plenty done but Melissa's going to kill me. She says I pay more attention to this place than to her.'

He never gets personal.

'Oh'.

My glass is nearly full, as is his. It's strange being in the office with just him. Disconcerting. But he also seems calmer. Less to prove with just me around, I suppose.

'Melissa should be happy you work so hard, Harry. But promise me one thing: when – if – you have a kid, don't leave her to do all of the skivvying at home. It's not sexy.'

He stares at me in surprise.

'You're kidding, aren't you? If we have a child she'll have an army of nannies and tutors around. My wife will not miss a stroke of her social life for a child. It will simply be something to dress up, like her Pomeranian.'

I actually spit wine when he says this. He chuckles. His laugh is warm. I'm not sure I've ever heard his real laugh before.

'If you ever repeat that I am a dead man.'

I only recently noticed the sadness. I always thought he was just arrogant, but there's definitely pain in those eyes. Even when he laughs. He seems younger when he's not angry. About thirty-six, I'd guess. And now that I'm looking, you can tell he keeps fit. His body's probably very taut under those clothes.

Jesus. Where did that thought come from? Especially about Harry. But then, the truth is I am hormoned up to the max since my night of juvenile passion with Philo and I am running on a combo of alcohol nights and coffee days, with a few carbs in between to stop me from dying. So all in all I'm pretty much insane.

I open my gob unexpectedly.

'I won't repeat it. My fella's got an obsessed fan at work and he copped off with her the other night. So right now, I think all relationships are basically shit.'

He actually guffaws.

'I shouldn't laugh. That is terrible, Alice. But you do have a way of putting things.'

'Thank you. And please don't pass that information on, especially to Belle. I can do without the false sympathy.'

'Um? Exactly when do you think I started pouring my heart out to the office gossip?'

'Just making sure. Bet she'd love to hear that my relationship is wobbling. Make her feel better about her own life.'

'Have you two split up?'

'Having a rest from each other would be a better way of putting it.'

I neck the rest of my drink.

'But right now he's looking after Barney and I have to go and relieve the cheating skunk of his responsibilities and kiss my sleeping son good night.'

He looks at the bottle then at me.

'I'll just have to finish this on my own then. Thank you for your hard work. And thank you for smoothing things over with the Mayfair people, they sound very happy.'

'I know. I'm a genius!'

He nods and pours another drink for himself. I move to leave.

'Oh, and Alice? I like your hair. And your shoes.'

'Thank you.'

Slightly flustered by his complements I wave my fingers at him and exit, collecting my bags of booty from the coat cupboard on the way out.

CHAPTER FOURTEEN

It's dark out here but not cold. I like walking on my own, watching people pass by on their way here and there, smelling of strong perfume and lager and fags. I consider hailing a cab but, aware that I'm not Bill Gates and I've already spent more than enough today, I hop on a bus and get out my book. The luxury of taking my time is delicious. Barney will already be asleep and I don't have to rush home for Tommi. He's never rushed for me. And just considering how many times he hasn't rushed home and it maybe hasn't been for work reasons and I've been sitting there, dinner in the oven for him, wine out and telly on like an obedient old granny, makes my blood turn to steam. So I stop considering it. I think of Harry and his wounded eyes and the pleading in his voice to his wife. Maybe he's not such a dick after all. Everyone seems to have a story. Why are so many of the stories sad?

Amateur psychology is a dangerous thing but I'm now starting to believe that all relationships are a minefield of shitty compromise. Even if Rabbit Face hadn't texted and Tommi hadn't been up to anything, I was still unhappy. If I wasn't unhappy I wouldn't have been so receptive to Philo surely? And I wouldn't have been admiring the light hairs I could see on Harry's chest tonight, after he loosened a couple of buttons on his shirt.

My phone rings. I already texted Tommi so it shouldn't be him. Maybe it's my mum? But when I look at the screen, it's Talia. I haven't spoken to her or Geoff since Tommi 'moved in' to their house. I've hardly spoken to anyone. I'm quite scared to answer.

'Hello?'

'Hi Alice, how are you?'

Her voice is like expensive bourbon. All dark and smoky. I sometimes wonder if she puts it on to sound sexy. I'll bet she does.

'I'm well. You know, a bit disorientated but fine.'

'Good. Right.'

'You okay?'

'Yes, fine. Where are you?'

'On the bus from work. Got a big job on this week.'

The phone goes quiet for a few seconds. This is bloody weird. I wish I hadn't picked up.

'Right. Well, sorry to bother you. It's just, well I spoke to Tommi to see what time he's coming home, I mean here, tonight and he seems terribly upset. I know you two… I know there's a problem but don't you think you could talk it out? He loves you so much and Barney needs his daddy as well as his mummy.'

I feel a stab of pique. She's coming across as patronising with a side order of accusatory. Like I've sent Tommi away for no good reason, simply to upset Barney.

'You do know he cheated, right?'

'Well, I know there was a drunken incident, yes. And I'd be furious if Geoff did it. I'm not denying that.'

'Yes, well, it seems to me there may be more to it than one drunken incident. His mad-as-a-box-of-spiders girlfriend contacted me. He has been round her flat since. That doesn't sound like a one-off to me.'

Many of the houses I'm passing on residential streets are lit up, with blinds and curtains open. Lots of little domestic set-ups with granddads, uncles, dads, mums, young families, dogs, parrots, spinsters and widowers. All in little time capsules of their own, all making their own stories.

Talia sighs down the line.

'Well, I don't know about that, Alice. But I'm sure this girl is a little infatuated with him, which is understandable, isn't it? He's a lovely man. Maybe he went round to tell her it could never be. I know he did wrong... but there have been mitigating circumstances, haven't there?'

Did I just hear right?

'Not mitigating in the "he should be allowed to mess around whenever he likes" way. But, you know, we've had coffees and stuff when you've told me you've found other people attractive or that you're tired of just being a mum. Maybe he got the feeling you were tired of him and he - '

'Talia, the things I told you, the things I said about my relationship and my life, were just day-to-day grumbles. I told you them in confidence to get them off my chest. Not to do anything about them. I never did anything about them.'

'No. But you've been depressed a lot. I know it's post-natal. But I got that too and I struggled through it. I didn't, you know.'

I look around me. The man behind me has his iPod on. I can hear some kind of horrendous kiddie-techno pinging out of his little ear buds. The old lady two seats in front seems to be oblivious. I put my mouth closer to the receiver anyway and lower my voice.

'What? Let it drag on? Funny that. With your paid-for house and your personal trainer who got you back in shape within months of giving birth. And the way the lines on your forehead and chin disappeared after a little visit to your "doctor". Then there are all of your holidays, and the way you and Geoff still get time on your own because you can afford help, and the way you can choose your own work hours. I can see how things must have got on top of you and how you must have struggled through. Well done you.'

'Alice! There's no need to be spiteful. I'm just saying, Tommi has been a good partner. He messed up this once. Surely you can give him a chance, for Barney's sake if nothing else?'

'Jesus, Talia. If I wasn't giving him a chance I would have told him to get out and never come back! I didn't. I'm simply having a bit of time on my own to think, that's all. But he's so used to being looked after he can't hack it. He's a great big bloody baby. And, as for Barney, I happen to love my son with all of my heart, so stop brandishing his name like a sword. I wouldn't care but your two have a nanny on hand night and day while you do whatever you want. She even looks after your fucking goat! If Tommi's such a brilliant partner then you have him, it certainly sounds like you fancy him, you condescending twat.'

And on that thoroughly immature note I end the call and spend another fifteen minutes breathing slowly and fighting the urge to call her back and shout, 'FUCK YOU!'

CHAPTER FIFTEEN

Never did I think I could feel this good in a skirt. One that's not long and floaty and matched up with flat boots, that is. What a moment to savour it was when I tried on all of my new gear and everything fit, except the dresses which were huge and made me look like a psychedelic tent, and one little vest top which said it was a size twelve but was actually a six or something and almost cut off my circulation. Everything else worked. Elen all but gave me a round of applause when I showed up at work in my new boots with tight black jeans and a fitted satin shirt. This, coupled with my new hair, a big turquoise pendant and an old pinch-waisted tweed jacket from my student days, made me look like a new woman. One with a shape. A curvy, pleasing shape. I even did the eyeliner with gloss thing that Elen had showed me. It feels like a two-finger salute to things going wrong in your life when you dress to feel good. I stalked into work like I belonged there, like they needed me. Not like I'd woken up at four o'clock in the morning, bawling my eyes out. Again.

Several outfit combinations later and here I am in the school playground on a Friday morning in a new red shirt, debuting my pencil skirt with black hold-ups and the cherry shoes that still haven't pinched my toes yet, although I do have a plaster on my heel where they rub. I'm not sure I can wear hold-ups too often as they make me feel like a slut, all of that air up my skirt, but they were on offer and I wanted to see how they felt as I've never worn them before. I can tell I'm walking differently as I take Barney to class then sweep him up in my arms for the biggest hug in the world, which he struggles out of because it's 'not cool'. He does take my hand fleetingly though and squints up at me.

'You look pretty, Mummy.'

I almost tear up again. He's been withdrawn because of me and his daddy. And he had a meltdown this morning because he didn't want to put on his shoes. I know he senses that something is seriously wrong but I just don't quite know what to say. I've told him that everything will be okay and that Mummy and Daddy just had a row and they're 'cooling off'. But he keeps asking if we're 'cool enough' yet? I think he heard me after I got home from work on Monday. I told Tommi in no uncertain terms that he wasn't coming back yet and his friends weren't going to bully me into it. I was furious with Talia, pissed off she was taking sides, and pissed off that I'd become so infantile on the phone. Tommi left looking terrified and said he would do 'anything it takes' to prove he loved me. I told him he could 'stop visiting his girlfriend' for a start.

I really hope Barney didn't hear that bit.

I bend down to Barney and hug him again. I whisper in his ear.

'Remember, Grandma is coming to pick you up from school. She's got a new film for you and some treats. I'll see you back at home after work.'

He juts out his chin.

CHAPTER FIFTEEN

'Why are you staying out again?'

'Just work, sweetheart, but that'll get you your new bike for Christmas, won't it? All of this money I'll be earning!'

His face lights up.

'I want a big boy's bike!'

'I know you do. Now make sure you don't have too many sweets tonight or you'll be sick.'

'Grandma likes me to eat her sweets. She says it keeps her slim.'

'Does she now?'

My mother comes from the same world of 'ply kids with sugar and they will love you' as Tommi's mum. Every few weeks she comes over to stay for a night, sometimes for two. Supposedly it's to give me and Tommi a break but I wind up spending most of my time chatting with her and if I do go out with Tommi it's usually for food and a bottle of wine and we're stuffed and falling asleep by ten-thirty.

My dotty but lovely mum likes to get the train into London from Hemel Hempstead. My parents moved there when they retired. She brings magazines to read and a salad sandwich. She still gets perms and wears peach blusher and everyone chats with her on the train. They moved to Hemel Hempstead apparently because they wanted to be in the countryside but still close enough to see their grandchild. At the time they hoped we would multiply Barney into grandchildren, I think, but I sincerely doubt that is going to happen now. Anyway, they're happy enough with their little cottage and their garden. So much so that my dad hardly leaves it and I have to take Barney to him. I don't mind though because it's peaceful there and Barney adores this funny, kind man who teaches him to plant sweet peas.

I have told my mother nothing of what has been going on, except that Tommi and I have had an argument and he won't be around when she comes over. She didn't say much. I'm sure she'll say plenty later. Tommi's going to see his best mate from school tonight, as far as I know (he's never shown much interest in show-off Bob over the past couple of years and for all I know it's a cover story for seeing Rabbit Face) but then he's coming for Barney tomorrow and taking him to his mum's again for the night. I reckon he'll have to tell her what's going on soon, as it's the second time he'll have gone there without me. He won't enjoy that. And I'm sure he'll sell it so that I look like the bad guy.

I turn away from the classroom and sashay my way to the gate (well, not quite sashay, but I can't stomp in these shoes like I did in my Uggs). As I move I get a whiff of my new perfume, which I popped on the emergency card the day before yesterday and which smells of amber and vanilla. I like to think it wafts around me like a cloud of mystery. I decide, as I reach the gate, that no matter what it takes I shall fulfill my promise to Harry tonight. It has become my personal goal to finish everything I said I would and prove to him once and for all that I'm the best at my job in that bleedin' office.

As I exit the school, I happen to glance up and my eyes lock with a pair of hot coals in a suntanned face. Christ, it's 'Sexy Dad'. And he's staring.

'Sexy Dad' is my nickname for a guy in his forties with close cropped greying hair, a permanent five o'clock shadow and a jawline and cheeks of chiseled perfection, who is father to a pretty little girl in Barney's year. He's one of those people who makes his fitted jumpers, jeans and suede sneakers look very, very expensive. Knowing this school, which has a mix

CHAPTER FIFTEEN

of working-, middle- and upper-class children, there's every chance that they are really, really expensive. But this guy has style anyway, full stop. He has to be Italian. Everything about him screams 'Italian'. But then, what would I know. I only stopped dressing like a Greek widow in the last fortnight.

Either way, he's very gorgeous, even if he is really quite short. There are obviously plenty of attractive, if knackered-looking, dads around but he is like an emerald in a pile of green wine gums. (Wine gums are great and quite tasty but emeralds are sparkly and special, if you see what I mean.) And now I've caught him looking at me and I am perplexed. I don't think he has spared me a glance before, not in all the time Barney's been at school.

Thank God I have the presence of mind not to trip over. I smile faintly and nod as I keep walking at as fast a lick as I can in these shoes. He nods back. His smile is also slight, but it's there. I have no idea why I've become so fond of men's approbation; it shouldn't matter if blokes are suddenly giving me appreciative glances, but it does, it bloody does. I wonder if wearing colourful tops instead of black is doing this to me. Right now, I am basically skin, bones and raging hormones, with wine flowing through my veins.

I resist the urge to check behind me as I reach the street, to see if he's still looking. That would make me the biggest dork in history. But I can't help a little thought of him as I stand on the crowded tube trying not to inhale in the breath of the guy next to me. It smells like cowpat. I wonder if he's cleaned his teeth. I'm eating a bit more this week, mostly because I wouldn't be able to work so hard if I didn't, so I had some muesli for breakfast, thank goodness, or I would be retching. I turn my head away as much as is polite and I think of 'Sexy

Dad' and how he always drops his daughter off at school on his own. I've never seen a wife or partner. Maybe she works or maybe he's a single dad?

For a ridiculous second, I imagine Barney with a new sister, living with me and 'Sexy Dad' and going off on adventures. Then I bring myself up short and feel as guilty as I've ever felt. That is so shitty, to Tommi and to Barney. What is the matter with me? Today I shall plough my mind into the task at hand, stop thinking nonsense thoughts about sexy men and return to my mother tonight, victorious about my completed work, and ready to face a chat about my future with Tommi. I know she will tell me to take him back immediately and make it work for Barney. I know that for sure because she loves both of my boys and she believes that relationships are for keeps where children are involved.

Somewhere inside I believe that too.

CHAPTER SIXTEEN

The best laid plans and all that. My own client, who had been happy as Larry with my work so far, called at eleven in the morning and wanted me to change something. That something being the whole bloody concept of the plan I'd given her on Thursday. She said she'd 'had a dream' that the feng shui of the office would be wrong and wanted everywhere to be more open and airy and for the theme to be more 'nature-based'. I wanted to tell her that I felt she was full of shit and maybe she should have a reality check. But of course I couldn't.

This rather knocked me as now Monday and Tuesday were going to be a nightmare. Change of concept or not, the deadline still stood. So I tried to rush the extra job I'd taken on, then that went to pot when the client asked for 'another meeting just to clarify'. The meeting ate up a lot of the day and involved me trying to flatter and placate a senior female boss who'd obviously had a crush on Hass and wanted the same attention from me. Hassan was the best arse-licker on the planet. Only my determination to prove I could get the job done prevented me from blowing a fuse. The most annoying thing was, I couldn't join her in a wine-sodden lunch, which would have made life easier, because I had too much to do.

So, eight thirty at night and mission is not accomplished. I will have to tinker all weekend and hopefully get it ready by Monday afternoon. I am in the office alone, I've already called and said goodnight to Barney and I am feeling very deflated. It's dark and I've been working by the light of my desk lamp. When my mobile rings I don't expect the shrill noise and almost fall off my chair. It's Harry. He never calls me outside of working hours. I pick up.

'Have you gone home yet?'

'No.'

'Have you finished?'

'No. I'm sorry. I'm going to have to do some of this in my own time. It should be finished by Monday afternoon, I hope.'

'That's fine. You should be at home relaxing by now, anyway.'

He's changed his tune.

'I know. I'm going to shut up shop in a minute.'

'Good girl. And thanks for everything.'

Is he drunk?

'You're welcome.'

My eyes are stinging. I rest my head on my forearms on the desk in front of me. My mind whirs as always. I just wish everything was simple. I would have had the work wrapped up by now if people weren't such total cretins. But of course the world isn't perfect; there's always a spanner waiting to jump in and mess things up. Spanners at work, spanners in your hopes, spanners in your relationships.

I don't even think of Rabbit Face as a spanner anymore. There's more to that situation than Tommi's admitting and I'm going to get to the bottom of it. I need to talk to him properly. That's exactly what my mum's going to say, I know it. I'm dreading the 'you have to be responsible' talk from my

CHAPTER SIXTEEN

well-meaning but old-fashioned mother.

Right now my enthusiasm for all of this talking is nil. Not having Tommi in the house has mostly been nice. Is that bad of me? The routine has been easier. Surely I should be aching to have him back in my bed? Even the tears I sometimes shed in the night are for what my world used to be years ago with Tommi, and not what it became. My eyelids droop. This time last week I was off out dancing. I begin to drift in the quiet dimness of the office.

Suddenly I am woken by the main office door swinging open. I get such a fright as it bashes against the back wall that I let out a scream and grab the nearest paperweight to throw at the intruder, who emerges from the gloom and into the weak glare of my desk lamp.

Harry.

Harry, not in a work suit. Seeing the shock on my face, he bursts out laughing and my fear turns to confusion. He has two carrier bags in one hand and holds up a set of keys in the other and jingles them. Then he closes the door behind him.

'Sorry to disturb you, Alice, but I thought you deserved dinner.'

'You scared the life out of me.'

He rattles the carrier bags. What's he doing here?

And now I can smell it. Chips. There are proper chip-shop chips in one of those bags. My stomach lurches. I realise I'm very hungry.

'Dinner in the boss's office!'

He motions me to follow him. Inside his room he switches on a wall lamp which is made up of lots of tiny lights on metal tentacles. It has a dimmer switch and is very pretty. I can't do this, my mother will be waiting.

'Harry...'

He is moving things off his heavy mahogany desk and into its roomy drawers. Pretty quickly it's cleared. He puts down a bag and opens it, taking out two separate portions of chips in polystyrene holders with little wooden forks. I can smell the vinegar. My stomach groans again.

'I've got to get home.'

'Isn't Tommi babysitting?'

'No, my mum is.'

'Well, can't you tell her that you are having a quick bite to eat then coming back? I'll pay for a taxi for you. How about that?'

I don't know what's going on here. Why isn't he at home? Apparently he and his wife have a very nice apartment in a posh square about ten minutes from here, plus a country house, too. Surely they have functions and dinner parties to attend? As for my mother, she'll be into one of her Catherine Cookson DVDs by now. She absolutely loves those old romance films but my dad hates them, so she comes to my house and she settles down after Barney's in bed, then breaks open the Milk Tray. Harry opens the other carrier bag and reveals a very good bottle of champagne. The bottle is dripping with condensation. It must be nice and cold. I begin to salivate.

'A thank-you for working so hard?'

The fizz has clinched it for me. I sit down and he smiles. His smile is lopsided. His cheeks are ruddy and his hair looks a little damp.

'Have you been to the gym?'

'Tennis. Tennis on Fridays. Tennis, shower, then a quick drive home to watch Sky Sport with a couple of beers. Got the house to myself until eleven or so. Depends what time my wife's dinner date finishes. But then I saw a light on in here so I gave you a little buzz. Just to make sure it was you and we weren't being burgled.'

He must be a member of some swanky gym nearby. How can anyone afford to be a member of a gym right in the middle of town? And did he really have to drive down this street to get home? I wonder if he's a bit neurotic about this office.

'These chips smell lovely Harry, thank you.'

Just for a moment he looks down and I could swear his cheeks grow ruddier.

'You're welcome. Tuck in!'

He exits and comes back with a couple of John Lewis champagne flutes from the kitchen. Mr Benham provided a job lot for visiting clients. He pops the cork and pours as I eat a couple of chips. They're divine. Then he joins me. Instead of sitting opposite, like he's about to give me a lecture, he pulls his chair to the side of the desk so he's sitting closer. His shirt is light, cream-coloured linen. My glass empties faster than my polystyrene plate. After about half of the chips I'm full. But happy enough to get a top-up of fizz.

'Harry, this feels odd.'

'Does it?'

'It's really nice of you but it just feels…'

He puts down his fork.

'A bit set-up?'

'Sort of.'

He looks away, then back again, and apart from embarrassment I see relief.

'I can't lie. I wanted to see you.'

Usually this would come in at about number six hundred on the 'things I'd expect him to say' list.

'Really..?'

'Sorry. Bit too in your face?'

'Well. Until last week you hated my guts and I thought you were a total twat.'

He starts to laugh again.

'Beautifully put.'

'But you did! You've been horrible to me ever since you got here.'

'You've treated me like a stupid upstart since I got here.'

'No, I haven't.'

Have I?

'You and your little mate snickering at me and taking the micky out of how I speak. I've felt like a fool in your presence since day one. Plus you've always been a bit of a miserable cow. Then, out of nowhere, you got very funny and dressed all, well, different and spoke to me like a person, and at one point, I believe, threatened me with mortal violence, and as a result became… more real. And rather more attractive. I mean, how does someone basically turn hot as hell overnight? It's ridiculous. You've bamboozled me.'

And as he says it I feel myself getting really flustered. I had no idea that was how I was coming across. I mean, come on. A miserable cow?

'I was not a miserable cow. Just a bit down.'

'Whatever. All I know is, you suddenly sparked up. The look in your eye is positively murderous. And let me tell you, it's damned sexy.'

'Is it?'

He stands, obviously uncomfortable at revealing too much and clears away the chips and polystyrene plates and wooden forks, loading them back into the carrier bag and taking them to the kitchen bin. When he returns he lingers by the door.

'I'm sorry, Alice. I've been very inappropriate.'

'No, you haven't.'

I stand too. I'm getting that feeling in the pit of my stomach again. Probably a good time to leave.

'Honestly?'

I can't read the look on his face.

'Chips and champagne. Good combo.'

'We haven't finished the champagne yet.'

My glass isn't empty. I drain it. He crosses to the desk until he's level with me and picks up the bottle. Condensation flies as he holds it up; the light through the green glass shows it to be half full. A cold droplet hits my skin, landing right in the hollow of my neck. He sees it. Then with unexpected boldness he leans forward and licks it off with the tip of his tongue. Such a cheeky move knocks all thoughts out of my head. He then swiftly kisses the place he just licked, lifts his head and backs off slightly.

'Sorry...'

I can't speak for a moment. Heat.

'That is definitely being inappropriate, Harry.'

'I know.'

'What the hell is going on with you?'

I should leave right this minute. But instead, I hold out my glass for a refill. He duly tops it up.

'I think I'm going a little mad. I should go home.'

'Should you?'

I'm feeling rather dangerous again. It's the fizz, obviously.

Our faces grow closer as he carefully perches on the edge of the table, eyes never leaving mine. Slowly, I take a sip of my drink and put my lips to his. Why am I behaving like a slut? Without missing a beat his mouth slightly opens and I let the cool liquid slip onto his tongue. He swallows and a kiss ensues.

Against my cheek he whispers, 'I have never come across a sexier place from which to drink champagne.'

I take another sip of my drink and while my lips and tongue are cold I kiss where his ear meets his neck. I hear his intake of breath as I kiss down to his throat.

I'm well aware I have no excuse for this extraordinary behaviour, I'm not even drunk. And worse still, I can't seem to stop.

I don't protest as his hands grip the backs of my thighs through my skirt and pull me closer to him, not even when the material begins to ride up. Beneath the bunched-up material my hold-ups are holding up, pushing the extra flesh into the thigh version of muffin tops. If he can feel them he doesn't say anything, he just brings those emboldened lips against mine and kisses me with more purpose than before. This is a Harry I don't recognise from work.

Without warning he brings up his hand and unfastens the shirt button at my cleavage. What I really should be thinking (and saying) is 'stop this, you're married, I'm out of control, and this is all wrong.' But what I'm actually thinking is, thank God I put on this nice, new, extremely reasonably priced indigo satin bra with matching pants instead of that too-tight lacy thing with ill-matching cotton belly-warmers.

Taking my lead, he takes a sip of his drink, leans forward and kisses my neck. As he does so he lets champagne drip from his mouth down my skin, eliciting a gasp from me. Then he looks up, eyes sparkling with mischief.

'I think I'd better get that...'

CHAPTER SIXTEEN

I nod, burying my hands in his hair, as he undoes two, three more buttons and licks away the droplets that are running down my ribcage. I have a fleeting thought about my soft, untoned belly, but that is swept away when he finishes unbuttoning, pulls my shirt apart and lets out a groan of appreciation as he brings his mouth to the satin of my bra, causing my nipple to stand to attention. I take his face in my hands and pull his mouth to mine again as he brings his hands to my backside and pulls me closer. I can feel his hardness as we kiss and feel my own heat building as he drags the rest of my skirt up and digs his nails into the flesh between my hold-ups and knickers.

'Jesus Christ, Alice... Look at you –'

I kiss him again, to stop his words. I want him inside me, right this minute. But I can't... Of course I can't...

He pulls away from me so he can drag my skirt up at the front and look at my hold-ups. Then he slides even further forward on the mahogany table pushing his hardness against my, by now, very damp underwear. Kissing him, I quickly undo his shirt. I place my hands on his skin, feeling his soft chest hair and broad shoulders. I move my hands to his belly. He is not thin and wiry like Philo. He is bigger, with more meat on him.

For a moment I stop to savour the feel of him and he takes both of my hands.

'Do you want to stop?'

I shake my head. 'Not yet.'

I kiss him again, then I burrow into his neck, breathing him in. Through the shower gel, I can smell his skin. Sweet, with a tang of something else. Something earthy. I move my lips to his chest, his nipples, then his belly as he supports himself on his hands. When I reach his trouser top I look up and his soft eyes show longing as well as fear. I understand that fear. But I know how nice a fear it is and, now kneeling, I smile at him as I undo his button and fly. He is wearing white boxers. I pull them back to reveal his cock which is hard and smooth and much like the rest of him, very nice to look at. Unable to stop myself, I take him in my mouth and he groans and drops his head back. His gasps become less controlled as I take him closer and closer to the edge, but well before time, he stops me. This is quite a surprise as Tommi has always been obsessed with blow-jobs and I have managed to get myself out of many an unwanted morning session by learning to be very adept with my mouth. But Harry isn't Tommi and evidently doesn't want to finish yet. He slips off the table and joins me on the carpet, tucking himself back into his boxers and kneeling so that we're facing each other.

'Why did you stop me?'

His hands plunge into my hair and he grips it tightly as he pulls my mouth a little bruisingly to his and whispers into my lips, 'My turn...'

Before I know it my back is on the floor and Harry, arrogant, annoying, clean-scrubbed, filthy as hell Harry, has taken his face down to my thighs, pushed my bunched-up skirt a little higher and is cascading kisses onto the hot, expectant skin revealed between my lace-top hold-ups and my knickers. I would normally be quite conscious of my ample thigh flesh being on open display but right now I'm way past caring. This man obviously likes what he sees, so who am I to argue? After a minute or two of me suffering the glorious agony of his lips avoiding the main attraction, suddenly his nose and mouth are against the satin of my pants and he is slowly exhaling his hot breath into the damp fabric, giving an almost unbearable blast of heated air to an already burning-hot place. Then, when I'm actually about to climb the walls, I feel his fingers yank my knickers to one side and all at once his tongue is there, moving insistently against me then reaching inside.

Christ, I have never felt anything like this. The fact that he's my boss, the fact that we're at work on the floor, the fact that I've not let Tommi do this in a long time, the fact that we won't suddenly have a six-year-old standing over us clutching his latest Lego creation… it all seems to be adding to the volcano inside me. It's almost too much to bear as I feel myself moving against his tongue, trying to keep some kind of control but failing and hearing nothing but a loud siren and then as the volcano bursts realising that the loud siren is – was – me. Not knowing quite how I'm suddenly covered in sweat and sobbing. Bloody hell, I've orgasmed and burst into tears. Ridiculous. I try to stop but it's too late.

'Alice?'

I bat away as many salty drops as I can, sit up and swallow.

He scrambles up too and puts his palm on my cheek.

'Did I upset you?'

'God, no. I'm just feeling a little insane.'

'Thank goodness for that, I thought I'd done something wrong.'

'No, no. You did everything right. I just… I shouldn't have let that happen. Sorry.'

'Don't be sorry. We both did it. I should be sorry but I'm not.'

I pull my skirt down to a more respectable length. After a moment or two my composure returns.

'I don't know how the hell that just happened.'

And I really don't. I had no intention of doing anything with Harry. In fact, until recently I thought he was a total idiot. Now I've had his cock in my mouth and suddenly I realise that if Rabbit Face is a cock-sucker then I am, too. No more moral high ground for me.

'I do.'

He snakes his hand over my ribcage and up to my bra. To my shock I immediately feel a renewed pulsating in my groin. What the hell?

'You are a sexy, gorgeous woman and I'm not sure I can be left on my own with you ever again.'

'What about your sexy gorgeous woman at home?'

He shakes his head but doesn't say anything.

'Are you guys…?'

'Isn't it bad form to talk about that stuff when you're having such a nice time?'

'No. If you're here with me now, something must be a bit awry at home, right? Or are you just bored?'

That sadness again, crossing his face like a rain-cloud.

'The last thing my home life is, is boring. It's more like the Battle of Waterloo. I'm the French.'

Something makes me want to ruffle his hair.

'I'm going to have to go. My mum is going to worry.'

'Yes. I'd better go too. If the wife gets back before me I'll be in trouble.'

The wife. Holy guacamole. I'm an unsisterly cliche. And that's two men now. Surely I should have got over this kind of misbehaviour in my twenties. But then, I didn't misbehave at all in my twenties, did I?

'Harry.'

He strokes his hand down my bra again.

CHAPTER SIXTEEN

'Yes?'

'We can't do this again, right?'

'We shouldn't. Not so sure about can't.'

'No, really. No-one is to know about this and we can't do it again. You're married, I'm half married.'

'I won't tell anyone, Alice. I'm not a bloody teenager. But as for not doing it again. If you really mean that, then I'll have to live with it, won't I?'

He doesn't sound very convinced or convincing.

'Say it like you mean it.'

'Okay, okay. Come here.'

He kisses me. I'm supposed to get up and leave now. I can't, it's a matter of pride. Instead, I kiss him hard and his hand strays back inside my F-cup. The heat returns like I didn't already just come. This time I'm not going to let him stop me as I move down and take his cock from his pants. I hear his moan of surrender as I close my mouth around him once more. With his shirt open, leaning back on his elbows, he looks like a different person. A proper, virile man, not a stressed-out, angry boss in a suit. He loses control very quickly and I can't help feeling proud that he comes so soon. As I grab my glass and take a gulp of champagne, he lays back on the floor, his face peaceful and flushed. I feel a rush of something as I look at him...

Stop it, stop it. You can't start caring about him. He's married.

As I straighten myself up ready for the journey home, he opens an eye.

'You do realise, you just ruined my life?'

I laugh.

'A one-off gesture. Now we have to be good again.'

'It will take all of my strength not to throw you against the filing cabinet on Monday, you filthy woman.'

'I'm probably going to be mortified on Monday.'

'Don't be. You've made my year.'

I now have to get in a cab and act in front of my mother like I didn't just have my boss's face in my knickers. Jesus.

CHAPTER SEVENTEEN

My son is inordinately excited as I pack the basket with various 'no artificial flavours or colours' crisps and cereal bars, cheese sandwiches (he flatly refuses to eat anything other than thick white bread with butter, edam and thin-sliced tomatoes), water and fresh orange juice in bottles. Every time I think of being in the office with Harry, or the 'concerned' chat with my mother that followed after I spilled out of the taxi, (she said Barney had been crying because he wasn't seeing Tommi enough) I colour up with shame. My mum is a nice person and is usually in her own little world, but I knew she would need an explanation sooner or later. I just wanted it to be later. When I told her the barest details about me and Tommi having had a big row (I didn't mention Rabbit Face or asking him to leave, just that he'd stayed with friends a bit to give me some space) she went very pale and picked at a strand on the cuff of her sweater.

Predictably, she said she came from a time when people were in relationships for the long haul and they 'made it work' and that Barney could get very damaged by such upheaval. Fair enough; but I wondered if she'd be so forgiving if she knew what her beloved Tommi had been up to with Rabbit Face. Or that he'd 'cheated' before. Not that I was going to tell her. That would just make everything worse.

In fact, just to cheer her up this morning I informed her, all false jollity and smiles, that Tommi and I were taking Barney for a picnic today for lunch and she suddenly looked less grey around the gills and said, 'Give him my love, I'm sure you'll make things right.'

I don't know about making things right, but I know I can't make things better by doing very naughty things with Harry Percival in his office. Apart from anything else he is a married man and I am now worse than Rabbit Face because I recently found out what it's like to have someone mess around with my partner and I've now done it to someone else – though I won't be texting Harry's wife to gloat. On the contrary, having shat on my doorstep at work I am going to have to negotiate a careful path back to the professional relationship Harry and I are supposed to have. It doesn't help that I now find him atrociously attractive.

The park looks lovely today, as Barney skips beside me, singing a song he learned at school about daffodils. It's mild and the trees are proudly displaying their fading greens, bright reds and mellow oranges in the noontime sun. His hair has the usual unintentional quiff and, because I couldn't get him to wear his hat for love nor money (he says hats make his head itch), his head is open to the elements. He is so happy that we're all going out together, it makes me feel guilty and wistful. Barney spots Tommi before I do, sitting on a bench reading a newspaper in his big duffle coat. He runs to him shouting.

'Daddy! Daddy, let's do aeroplanes!'

And I see Tommi's mouth stretch into his usual lopsided grin as he sweeps him up and spins him. Then he stops and his eyes find mine.

CHAPTER SEVENTEEN

'Fortification!'

He points down to his giant duffle pocket and the neck of a bottle is sticking out. Wine.

'Oh, how very civilised!'

I give him a hug. It's warm and comfortable and his smell is familiar as well as surprisingly new. Like a bit of him was always elusive to me and now he is someone else. It's a disconcerting feeling. We sit on the bench together and Barney wedges himself between us, holding both of our hands.

'I like the flowers... I like the daffodils... I like the mountains... I like the rolling hills... and I like the fireside, when the lights are low... singing a doowapa-doowapa-doowapa-dooo...'

It's not difficult to learn as he sings it in his best, piping, wavery voice. I kiss his head and then add my own slightly discordant rendition.

'Do you want your picnic first or play first, Barney Boo?'

'Don't be silly, Daddy, I have to exercise to get properly hungry!'

Then Barney runs through the gate of the park and climbs the steps to the giant slide, waving to us as he reaches the top. I know of old that he'll probably do this at least twenty times. He loves that slide.

I'm left sitting rather uncomfortably with the man who is, to all intents and purposes, my husband. Even if we didn't sign anything to that effect.

'Hello.'

Without anything to prove in front of Barney, the smiley façade has drooped. He looks tired and when I offer him a sandwich he shakes his head and opens the wine. I'm not hungry either and I take out two green plastic beakers which he fills and we both gratefully sip.

'You look knackered, Tommi.'

He laughs into his cup, splashing wine onto his chin.

'Why thank you, Alice. You, conversely, look refreshed.'

'Early night and mum taking care of Barney. They watched *Toy Story* together this morning. I got an extra hour.'

Plus of course, I had a fabulous orgasm, did I not?

'Lucky you. I got the two terrors running up and down outside my room before seven shouting, "Is he up yet, Mummy?" I never thought I'd say this but I'm starting to hate those kids. Barney's much better.'

'Tommi! You can't say that.'

'Yes I can. I prefer the goat. I think he hates the kids too.'

'Doesn't sound much fun.'

He glances at me, then waves at Barney who has now befriended a blond-haired boy in green bobble hat and is making a train with him on the slide.

'It's not. I want to come home.'

'I know.'

'Alice, I need to know what's going on. I can't live there another minute and if you won't let me come home I'll have to rent a flat… and I can't pay my part of the mortgage and pay rent. It's impossible.'

Oh God. To be fair, I don't think I'd want to stay at Talia and Geoff's for very long either. It's not just the 'free thinking' way their children are brought up (mostly via the nanny) but because Talia is so used to being a control freak in every other area of her life, there's no way she won't be passive aggressively tapping Tommi up for information. And I know he hates that.

'Tommi… I always knew our house was too expensive.'

'It's not. It's not too expensive when we're both living there and contributing. It's only too expensive when you won't let me come home and I have to pay for somewhere else.'

Now he's looking flushed and frustrated.

'You say it like I have no reason to be distant from you.'

'We can put it right if you let me come back. I am well aware that I messed up. But nothing is going on between me and Em anymore. It was a one-off thing that grew out of us being friends and me being pissed. I now know I can't treat her as a friend because she wants more. I really am doing my best, but I need to know we have hope. Me and you.'

Barney is watching us from the roundabout. His bobble-hatted friend is pushing and Barney is looking at us as he spins. I smile broadly at him and blow a kiss.

Seeing absolutely no reason to lie, I put my hand on Tommi's sleeve.

'Tommi, as far as living arrangements go, you've had a shit deal. Sorry. I was so mad at you, I just wanted you out of my sight. But now that I've had time and space to think. I wonder if you'd be so eager to come home if you'd been able to live somewhere quiet and nice on your own. No-one telling you that what you're watching on TV is shit, or questioning what you're wearing or needing attention when you've already worked all day and taken care of Barney and you want to be left alone...'

'But... I don't think like that.'

'No. Because I don't do those things to you. You do them to me. I might nag and tell you off, but I also have to leave my job early every day to be there for Barney, I have to be a domestic goddess in the kitchen, take jibes about my dowdy outfits and be prepared to have sex when I'm so tired that all I want to do is curl up under the duvet with a book.'

It occurs to me as I'm saying this, how ironic it is that my sex drive has gone through the roof since he went from under it. I wonder what this means. He is looking more and more crushed.

'So having sex with me is just some horrible duty.'

'*No*. Having sex with someone when you're exhausted and feeling ugly, fat and overworked is a horrible duty. Do you realise, since you left, you've looked after Barney about five hundred per-cent more than you did before? And I've felt like a new person, just because I didn't have to be in a rush all of the time. We've actually shared the duties. And that's how it should always have been.'

'So you want me to live somewhere else so you get more leisure time?'

'No! No, it's something to think about. Why have I been doing everything on my own for so long?'

'Because you wanted to.'

'What?'

'You could have had all of this before. But Barney was born and then suddenly you weren't just his mother, you were mine. I didn't need another mother, Alice. That's not exactly sexy either, is it?'

I'm too stung to speak for a moment. He's right. I grab the bottle and top myself up.

Barney is coming down the slide again, giggling at his mate who looks like he's about to pull his trousers down.

'Until this happened you never offered to help me out, Tommi. Your job has always been more important.'

'I didn't think you even liked your job. And this isn't just about work, is it? Look at you, you've had your hair done, you've started dressing differently, you even walk differently.

CHAPTER SEVENTEEN

It's like you've suddenly blossomed since you got shot of me.'

'Maybe I'm just trying to compete with the Amazonian blonde you copped off with?'

'Don't.'

'Anyway, you never explained why you went round to her place last week. I don't even know the full extent of what's happened. You say you want us to talk, but you're so cagey when it comes to her.'

Like a ridiculous sign from the gods that is precisely when his phone begins to ring. The theme tune to *The Flintstones* blares out. When he pulls it out of his pocket, his face drops. On impulse I grab it off him.

It's her. I stare at him in shock and pass it back, still ringing.

'Oh my God. Are you seeing her?'

He kills the call and drops it in his pocket, puts his head in his hands.

'No, I'm not seeing her. That's why she's calling. She keeps calling and texting me.'

On cue his phone starts ringing again. He ignores it.

'At work she's friendly, too friendly. I don't go to the pub any more because she always tries to sit by me. I grab a sandwich and eat it at my desk instead. When I'm away from work she bombards me. When I went round there, it was to try to reason with her. She said she needed to talk to me and I thought it might help. What she really wanted was to convince me that we're made for each other. Do you really think I would risk messing around with her when I miss you and Barney so much? She's a lunatic, Alice, and I don't know what to do.'

His phone beeps a message. He looks at me and I see a lost child in his eyes. Just then Barney comes careering towards us, his bobble-hatted friend receding into the distance with his bobble-hatted mother.

'I'm so hungry I could eat *you*, Mummy!'

'You can't eat me, I didn't bring any ketchup!'

As he runs towards us he begins to chortle and I peck Tommi on the cheek.

'I'm sorry, it must be awful.'

'It is.'

He squeezes my knee. Barney looks delighted.

I fish one of his white-bread sandwiches from the basket. I can't believe he doesn't get bored having the same thing every time.

Maybe that's just me.

CHAPTER EIGHTEEN

I don't usually like Mondays much but I couldn't suppress a smile at Barney Boo's delight this morning when his dad set off for school with him. Tommi showed up at 8 a.m., as planned, looking like he'd had about six minutes' sleep. I was very impressed. He even helped Barney get dressed.

After a huge tussle in my head I've decided to allow Tommi to come back, on the proviso that he stays in the 'big' spare room for the time being as a 'housemate'. Then he won't be tortured by the two Tasmanian devils at Talia and Geoff's and won't have the money worry of having to get a flat. I'm still not sure what's going on in my noggin or what I really want, but I can't lock him out of his own house forever. Though, when I told Suze and Smithy of my plan last night, Smithy shouted 'let him stew a bit more, at least!' before Suze could wrestle the phone from him. I told Tommi just before he and Barney marched off together this morning and he looked so relieved I thought he might cry. I have to be fair here, I can't be selfish. And I do love him.

We have two spare rooms, the 'big' spare room and the 'sweet' spare room. The big one is en-suite but the sweet one, though smaller, overlooks the garden and is the one my mum always uses because she says it's cosier. She likes to sit at the mini dressing table and admire our rose bushes as she primps her perm. Actually I've gone even more off this flippin' house now. Ever since I saw Elen's flat, it's hit home how much I like a place with character and not too many rooms to clean. Tommi hates the idea of bold colours on the walls and reconditioned furniture that I could get cheaply from auctions then sand and paint. He has always liked plain white walls and neutral carpets but it doesn't feel like 'me' at all. Whatever the hell 'me' is.

Right this moment, sitting at my desk, nursing a very hot cup of filter coffee, 'me' is a chastened and nervous slightly hung-over mother in a mustard shirt and coral lipgloss. I know, I know, who is this woman? I'm wondering when she'll feel brave enough to walk into her boss's office and give him a progress report on a pitch for a job in Hoxton. What have I done? Suddenly I'm too shy to speak to the man I only recently started getting along with. I am such an idiot.

As I check emails and generally procrastinate, a young woman enters the office. She is tall and elegant, her long hair has streaks of sunlight through it; she has healthy flawless skin and expensively cut jeans. Everything about her screams breeding and money. For one confused moment I think she must own the Hoxton place I'm trying to pitch our services to, but I can't fathom why the owner would be here. That's when she looks around the office, past Belle and my bedazzled co-workers and fixes her gaze on me. Her eyes are an amazing blue/green. I think they call it azure. No-one with a child could ever look like that. Not without tens of thousands of pounds worth of help and probably not even then. As she approaches I smile. I don't know what else to do.

CHAPTER EIGHTEEN

'Hi. Alice, isn't it?'

She has a sharp voice. Vowels made of knives.

'Yes, that's right.'

I stand up and offer my hand. She takes it with two fingers and a thumb. She's obviously not a hand-shaker.

'I'm Melissa. Harry's wife.'

My stomach sinks into my knees. I glance at his closed office door. He mustn't know she's here.

'Oh, hello Melissa, nice to meet you... How on earth do you know my name? I don't think we've met...'

I'd usually remember if I met a goddess. A much-younger-than-me goddess without a line on her face and a good six inches in height over me. I feel like an Oompa Loompa standing here. I perch on the edge of my desk, trying not to look embarrassed.

'No, but when I came to pick my father up from the office party last year, you were talking to him and I asked who you were as we left. He said you were one of his best workers.'

I can't believe what I'm hearing. Obviously he must keep closer tabs on his businesses than I thought. Best workers?

'Anyway. I just wanted to say thank-you for all the hard work you've been doing recently. You've helped Harry no end and he came home a very happy, if slightly drunk, man on Friday. Seems the company has kept to every deadline, despite the defection of their favourite designer...'

Her face pinches slightly as she says this. I don't care how pretty those eyes are, they're cold.

'Thank you, Melissa. But really, I'm just doing what your dad pays me for.'

'Yes.'

She stares at me for a fraction too long and I don't like

it. When she makes for Harry's office I'm extremely relieved. Belle looks around her screen and one over-made-up eye glints across at me. I smile innocently and retire to the loo, even though I don't need it. I lock myself in a cubicle for a few moments until my palpitations calm down. That was awful. When I leave the toilet stall I slowly wash my hands and reapply gloss. I so want her to be gone before I venture back out there. How did Harry end up with someone so intimidating? She's like flint.

As I powder my cheeks and nose, I am horrified when the door opens and in struts Melissa. She joins me at the mirrors and needlessly pulls a comb through her perfect hair.

'You've changed your style since last time I saw you, Alice.'

'Really?'

Does my voice sound high and strange?

'Yes. You're wearing more fitted clothes and you have a new hairstyle.'

'Well, a change is as good as a rest.'

Oh God, I'm talking like a weirdo. Princess Perfect is weighing me up in the mirror. This is really creepy.

'Anyone would think you were getting younger, not older.'

She sniffs. There's a definite edge there.

'No, Melissa. You're the one who looks about twenty. But we're all getting older.'

'Not me. I don't intend to get a single line on my face for the next thirty years.'

She sounds amused, like she knows she can do it. Suddenly I feel pissed off that people with money can do so much to remain youthful and beautiful while the rest of us just have to suck up the hell that is ageing. I wouldn't mind if they weren't so smug about it.

CHAPTER EIGHTEEN

'Well, good luck with that. And good luck with keeping those perfect little breasts perky once you have a child.'

I don't know why I just said that, it's outrageous; I think it takes us both by surprise. She stops preening and looks straight at me in the mirror.

'I won't be having a child.'

I wonder if Harry knows about this.

'Right. Well, probably best if you're planning on keeping those puppies pointing at the sky.'

Amazingly, a laugh barks out of her. And she stares at me again. I wish she'd stop it. I think it's time to leave. As I turn, her long fingers close around my wrist.

'I think my husband fancies you.'

I am thunderstruck. The look of shock on my face is real. Oh shit.

'What? That's ridiculous. Why are you saying that?'

She lets go of my wrist.

'I wanted to see if you flinched. If you'd flinched I'd have known and I'd have gouged your eyes out.'

Fuck.

'I already have a fella of my own and a child.'

'So? Younger, handsome boss. Get your best shoes and perfume on, get the rack on show...'

She glances disapprovingly at my F-cups. Cheeky mare. Like I can help it.

'Get you a leg up that ladder.'

Melissa isn't smiling, anymore. In fact there's a tiny trace of a tic in that perfectly tanned, creamy cheek.

'If I want to climb a ladder I get my boiler suit and work boots on. I don't need a fucking man to get me up there. Sorry you've been feeling so insecure, Melissa. Have a lovely day.'

LOVE BUTTON

When I get back to my desk I am fuming. Is it me or are women right fucking shits sometimes?

Am I a right fucking shit?

CHAPTER NINETEEN

Never have I spent a day in a worse mood. I had a pair of metallic lilac-rimmed laser beams trained on me most of the time I was in the office. Belle had smelled a major rodent and hardly let me out of her sight. As for Elen, she was on (pre-planned) two-day leave having a long weekend in Paris with her sister, the lucky duck.

So I went out for a longer lunch than I'm allowed, on my own, and my only interaction with Harry was a swift visit to his office where he looked over my plans and said, 'That all looks in order'.

He seemed as mortified as I was.

Then, a few minutes ago, just before 5 p.m. when I was set to leave (my night to get back for the minder), Harry passed my desk and dumped a few papers in my in-tray. Beneath the first sheet – a completely extraneous form that I didn't even need – was a small handwritten note:

Red Café at 5.30. Please? H x

I crumpled it as soon as I read it, then, thinking better of it, opened it back out, scribbled over it with a black marker then ripped it into tiny pieces. I wouldn't put it past Belle to go truffling in my wastepaper basket. Perhaps I'm being paranoid but I don't care. Now I'm going to have to make a phone call. I've always been careful not to be late for the childminder. She's called Marina. She's a very nice girl from Poland and usually it's been our policy, mine and Tommi's, not to pay for an extra hour as it's wasteful; plus it's not good parenting, leaving our son with a babysitter when he's been at school all day. But sod it, it's only this once. When I call her she is perfectly happy and says she can stay as long as I like, as they're about to watch a movie together. I'm so relieved.

Soon, I make a big show of getting my coat on 'to go home' and give everyone a wave. Then I nip out into the evening homeward-bound crowds and walk two streets to Red Café

I know why he's chosen this place, as it has a front part then a little hidden room at the back. If he'd chosen a wine-bar or caf that opened onto the street we couldn't guarantee that no-one we know would spot us. Especially someone as nosy as Belle. I grab a crappy newspaper after I pay for my cappuccino and make my way to a corner table in the back room. At the moment it's empty, as most people seem to prefer being out front next to the windows. I like the little vases dotted about in here, they're very rustic, but the abstract paintings on the walls are bloody awful. Nervously I read a report or two about the nasty things that are happening in the world, but don't really take them in. I keep glancing up at the doorway and looking away again, just hoping Harry isn't delayed as I really can't take the mick and stay here much after 6 p.m. For a start, Tommi will probably be showing up at home at around 7.30, clothes bag in hand.

Tommi.

Spare room or not, he'll be back in the house. Weirdly, I don't want to think about that.

CHAPTER NINETEEN

At 5.34 p.m. Harry's flushed, anxious face hurries through the door, followed quickly by the rest of him. He plonks down in front of me and runs a shaky hand through his hair.

'Do you want a drink? I have a tea coming.'

'No thanks, I still have this. And I can't stay long.'

'Oh. Right, of course. Barney.'

'Yes… erm… are you okay? You look a bit crazed.'

'Crazed? Yes, actually, I probably do'

He takes a breath and loosens his collar. 'God, I hate suits.'

The waitress arrives and puts down his tea. After she's gone he stares at me, turquoise eyes slightly bloodshot. I don't know if his weekend has been drunken or sleepless, but he certainly has a fevered sheen.

'Bloody hell, Alice, I'm so sorry Melissa showed up. I had no idea she was coming…'

'It's okay, I kind-of gathered it wasn't expected.'

'What did she want?'

'She came to thank me for helping you get the work done last week. That's what she said when she walked in. She said she'd seen me before at last year's Christmas party. I certainly would've remembered if I'd seen her. She's totally stunning.'

'Hm.'

I don't know what 'hm' means. He's lost in his own thoughts.

'Is that all she said? That she wanted to thank you?'

'No. She said that first then went into your office, then appeared in the loos when I was washing my hands. Had plenty more to say in there.'

Harry's ruddy complexion pales somewhat.

'Alice, this is terrible. She's so… She shouldn't have done that. She told me she'd popped in to check how the office was doing, on her dad's behalf. She's having dinner with him this evening. But it's bullshit. Charles knows the office is fine. I could've told him that. What else did she say to you?'

I'm not sure what I should reveal. Then it occurs to me that the truth might just be easier.

'She said I'd changed style since she last saw me. Said I was trying to hook you, to get myself "up the ladder"; said that she thought you might fancy me and that that was probably a result of me having my tits on show. I think that was pretty much the gist. Oh, and apparently if she thought we were having it off she would gouge my eyes out.'

'She said that?'

'Not in those exact words, but pretty much.'

'Christ, you must hate me.'

'No. I just don't know how you wound up with someone like that. I can only imagine it was the beauty and money!'

My joke falls flat. He looks crestfallen.

'She was a very sweet girl when I met her. Or I thought she was. We had lots in common. Her dad is self-made just like mine. And both of us were sent to private schools to make sure we got a better education than our dads got.'

Wow. I'd assumed Harry was from a posh family. He notes my surprise.

'My dad's a builder. A successful one. Only he doesn't pretend to be someone he isn't. And he didn't bring me up to think I'm better than everyone else. I thought she was the same. But she's basically a self-obsessed psychopath.'

He doesn't look like he's joking.

'Harry!'

'She speaks to me like I'm a piece of shit. I think she now realises she wants a proper blue-blood for a husband and not an oik in disguise. But she won't actually admit it because her dad likes me. Instead she just criticises me constantly. But, you see, even if I'm not up to scratch as a husband I'm her property and when she got back on Friday night I was happy, in fact I was whistling when she walked in. I think she expected me to fail in fulfilling Hassan's contracts and it pissed her off that I didn't.'

'Why? Why would she want you to fail?'

'I told you. She's mad. She wants my constant attention. I don't know why, probably so she can nag more. She wants me to fail because she does absolutely nothing productive herself. She wants me to fail because I'm out of her control when I'm working. She wants me to fail so her dad will think I'm a loser. The list is endless.'

'I don't understand why she's insecure. She's so beautiful.'

'That's the other thing. She asked who had taken over Hassan's contracts and I said you. She asked if you'd worked late with me and I said yes and that I'd bought you chips as a thank-you. She was so angry I thought she was going to punch me. Her jealousy is uncontrollable. I mean, I know I'm gorgeous but...'

I slap his arm.

'Erm. I think you'll find it's me that's gorgeous!'

He takes a sip of his tea.

'I know exactly who's gorgeous, Alice. In fact it's been rather difficult to shake off that Friday feeling...'

'Harry -'

'What?'

I have to stop him.

'Tommi is moving back into the house tonight. He'll be in the spare room, but he'll still be home. I - '

'Jesus. You're taking him back?'

'No! Well, yes, sort of but, you know. Taking it slowly. Plus, today was a wake-up call. We can't give Melissa any more ammunition, she's too shrewd. At least you can look her in the face and swear you didn't cheat.'

'Oh, come off it, Alice, we cheated. Whether I actually, you know. Well, that's a technicality.'

'A very important one to most people.'

'Yeah right.'

'And we were wrong to do what we did.'

'Are you telling me you didn't like it?'

He leans in closer and lowers his voice. 'You didn't enjoy me licking champagne off you or what my tongue was doing when you came in my mouth, right there on the office floor?'

It only takes two seconds for my underwear to start dampening.

'You know I did.'

'Alice...'

I feel my face inching nearer to his, feel his breath on my skin. I stop myself before I get close enough to kiss him.

'Harry. In another life, you know that I'd - you know.'

He sighs.

'I know.'

He looks so sad, I want to drag him into the toilets right now and kiss him better. Kiss him everywhere. But that's not allowed. You can't have it both ways; that's not how the world works. Currently, I really really wish it did work like that.

I stand and so does he. He gazes at me.

'Sometimes life just isn't fair.'

For another scary moment I think he might kiss me and I think I might respond. But he doesn't and I don't. I simply squeeze his hand then leave, feeling completely gutted, and

CHAPTER NINETEEN

head for the tube.
 It's drizzling.

CHAPTER TWENTY

Having Tommi home is strange but Barney is in seventh heaven. When he goes to bed he wraps his arms around my neck so tightly, I wonder fleetingly if he's trying to kill me. He kisses my face many times and then as he snuggles down we have our usual exchange, with a new twist.

'Night night darlin'.'
'Bonne nuit, Mummy.'
'Bonne nuit, Barney Boo.'
'This is the best night ever.'
'Is it, now?'
'YES! Love youuuuuuuu.'

Bless him. My mum and dad stayed together. They never really even argued. They met young and they loved each other and that was that; no insecurity for me at all as far as their relationship went. I can't imagine what all of this faffing around has been doing to Barney's head.

When I get downstairs, it's almost a shock to find Tommi, wine glass in one hand and remote control in the other, watching some documentary about the Hindenburg. He's in the orange armchair, the one I've since commandeered, in a chunky fisherman's jumper with his hair all over the place.

CHAPTER TWENTY

His grey eyes glance up slightly nervously as I walk into the room.

'I poured you a glass. A large one. Actually, it's more like a basin.'

Sure enough, there's a massive glass of wine on the little table next to 'my side' of the sofa.

'Wow. Are you planning on getting me extremely drunk?'

'I'm planning on getting myself extremely drunk. You might as well join me.'

Little does he know that since he's been away I have spent as much time curled up on his big chair as I have on the settee. I've 'spread out' so to speak. But I smile, sit where I always used to sit, and hold up my glass in salute.

Then I glance at the clock and try not to wince that it's nearly time for 'my' show. I'm a sucker for interior-decorating shows, always have been, and I've been able to watch whatever I like in the last few weeks, but Tommi hates those programmes and prefers documentaries and action movies. The only common ground we have is music. We both love watching music stuff on TV.

He sees my eyes go to the clock.

'Argh, sorry. I've taken over the remote. Is there something you want to watch?'

'Why don't I record it and we can switch this off for a bit? Put some music on?'

'Okay.'

His voice is small. He's scared. This is just odd. I press 'record' then switch off the box. I choose a quiet, unobtrusive track then sit back down again.

'Is it me or does this feel strange?'

He nods.

'This does feel strange. But good strange. I mean, I've missed you and Barney so much. What happened was so stupid. I don't want my family to break up over it. We've made such a great life together.'

Have we? Don't get me wrong. I count my blessings every day. I have a beautiful healthy son, a roof over my head and enough food. Plus wine of course. And those things are good things. But I'd have those things whether I was with Tommi or not. I've hardly noticed it, but over the past years my bond with Tommi seems to have eroded to the point that I've already grieved for the carefree couple we were before we became parents. I know that my current feeling of detachment is partly to do with being irresponsible and naughty for the first time in years. It can get addictive. And I also know that I've taken such a knock it will take a while to trust Tommi. But I have 'redressed the balance' and now I have at least to attempt to sort out our relationship, like a grown-up should. I have to try, right?

'Did you tell Emma you were moving back home?'

He looks at me warily then shakes his head.

'I'll tell her tomorrow. I try not to talk about anything but business with her, but this has to be done. I'm actually scared. At least she's stopped calling so much.'

'But you work with her. How can any of this get better when you see each other all of the time?'

'I don't know Al. I've been such a twat. And she's basically a loony.'

'You're a magnet for loonies aren't you? That's how you ended up with me.'

We both laugh but it's half-hearted. It's easy to see how Em became obsessed with her good-looking, charming colleague

CHAPTER TWENTY

and how he fell for the adoration. A bit of me can't believe Tommi was so weak, but then I've come to realise that people expect too much of each other in relationships. If your partner becomes like a noose around your neck, why wouldn't you seek easy affection elsewhere? As I think this, I have a flashback to Philo, the beautiful young musician who would be impossible to have as a partner but was delicious as a one-night gift to myself, a gift I would never have received if Tommi hadn't fucked up. I try not to think about Harry though. My feelings are so confused about him. A selfish, snatched hour of naughtiness could have cost me my job and lost Harry his marriage. For what his marriage is worth.

Stop it. No more Harry thoughts.

Suddenly Tommi reaches his free hand across to me, which I take. It feels familiar but also alien, touching him like that.

'You are the best kind of loony, Al. Thank you for letting me come home. It's great to be here and great to escape the house of torture. Though we will have to invite Talia and Geoff over to dinner at some point. To say thank you for being there for us…'

No way.

'What? You do know what happened with Talia?'

'I know she called you. She didn't tell me what she said.'

'Oh really. Well, she called to give me hassle for not thinking of Barney and for treating you badly. She was out of order. I all but told her to fuck off. We've not spoken since.'

'Jesus. She didn't say. Though she hasn't said much at all for the last couple of days. She's been holed up in her office. Geoff said she was feeling down. I sort-of wonder if she didn't want me to leave.'

'That's probably the most perceptive thing you've ever said.'

'Is it. Why?'

I laugh.

'Okay, maybe not that perceptive. I'm sorry, Tommi. They may have been your friends through this but they haven't been mine. She's shown her true colours and I've heard nothing from Geoff. The only mates I've spoken to are Smithy and Suze.

'Pffft. Was he sober enough to speak?'

'Hey, don't be horrible about Smithy. He's a good man and they've been good friends to me. At least they're not a pair of snobs.'

Tommi doesn't really mix that much with the few old friends that I have left. Never has. We've always ended up hanging out with his friends, mostly because mine live far away. But I'm sure that when the chips are down, I can't trust Talia as far as I can throw her. I can trust Elen far more than Talia and I haven't known Elen very long at all.

'Okay. Well maybe we'll let things die down first.'

'Tommi, she might never speak to me again, I sent her off with such a flea in her ear.'

'She was probably only trying to help. Just didn't approach it in the right way.'

'She was being nosy and accusatory. She gets everything in life on a bloody plate and thinks she knows everything.'

'Wow. She's seriously pissed you off, hasn't she?'

'Sorry. I don't suffer fools at the minute. If I want to have fun in my life, the first thing to do is cut out the dead wood.'

'Jesus!'

Tommi springs up, surprising me, as ever, with his height, and sits down next to me, pretending to take my pulse. He peers into my face.

CHAPTER TWENTY

'Who are you, and what have you done with Alice? This sounds like the old Alice... the one who liked getting arse-holed, sleeping in 'til noon and punching attendants on the Waltzer!'

'That was only once. He was spinning us too fast, I nearly flew out of the car.'

'I'm sure once was enough to make an impression!'

He's sitting rather close now. Probably too close for the first night back at home. I lever myself onto my feet.

'I can't believe I haven't cooked anything yet. Barney had already eaten with Marina and...'

'Cook schmook. Let's get an Indian.'

'On a Monday?'

'On a Monday. You're looking so skinny, you could probably do with a few takeaways.'

I think of Em at his work. Tiny little bum. Long thin limbs. Young peachy skin. He didn't seem that averse to skinny when it came to her.

He goes to fish out a takeaway leaflet. I top up our glasses. It's comfy to have someone to eat with. Though, of course, if he wasn't here I'd watch whatever I want, eat something small with some nice wine and go to bed with my book. Not the worst alternative.

Not good to linger on that.

CHAPTER TWENTY-ONE

So, at 6 a.m. I was awake, all hot and sweaty and with a mouth like a dirt box, with no pint of water by the bed. I always have water. What was I thinking? Luckily, the wine and food had hit me like a sedative so all I had done was sleep, not collapse into Tommi's arms. I did have vague recollections of a greasy kiss and a slight fumble but nothing else. Horribly, I'd woken up feeling like there were two large house bricks swimming in battery acid in my belly.

Tommi was face down on the sofa, having been too knocked out by the food and two bottles of wine to climb the stairs.

Welcome to parenthood.

Incidentally, this didn't happen at three a.m. after a crazy night of dancing. Oh no. I think the total body shutdown happened before 11 p.m. *That* is why I don't eat heavy food late, especially on a school night.

As damage limitation, I swallowed two paracetamols with a pint of freezing cold tap-water, followed by Gaviscon and soluble fizzy vitamins, then lay down for half an hour in my pyjamas, just so I could pretend I'd been to bed properly before I got up. After that, I had the hottest shower I could stand with my tingly mint shower gel and eucalyptus shampoo, then

CHAPTER TWENTY-ONE

made my hair as bouncy and shiny as possible with the big round brush. Last but not least I piled on the foundation so I looked alive and put on a nice bright dress and lipgloss. As I sorted my face I considered whether I was becoming a vain dick-head. But then I felt so much better, I put it down to necessary pampering.

This, along with steaming black coffee from my filter, has been enough to fool my body temporarily into thinking all is fine. By the time 7 a.m. comes I'm pretty much sorted and Barney is as surprised as I am to find me in the kitchen, raring to get his breakfast together. Tommi is still comatose and we don't disturb him. Weeks of two children screaming and poking at him in the morning have obviously taken their toll. (The good thing about this is he is now less likely to ask for a second child.)

Barney eats his Weetos at the kitchen table as I sit with him and drink my coffee.

'Barney Boo,'

'Yes, Mummy?'

'Do you ever wish Mummy could pick you up from school instead of Marina?'

'I wish that all the time.'

'Do you?'

He shovels in another spoonful of chocolatey cereal and some brown milk trickles down his chin as he nods.

'I miss you at school. And Daddy.'

I gulp coffee to clear the lump forming in my throat. I am a bad mother. Simple as that.

'I want us to go to that place for ice cream after school.'

'What place?'

'It opened up *ages* ago. The other kids in my class go all

the time. They have all kinds of crazy flavours. They even have... peanut butter!'

'Oh my goodness, *peanut butter*? What about bogeys and soil? Do they have that?'

Barney laughs so hard he gets wet crumbs of cereal all over the table. 'No, but they've got cheese and poo!'

Now we're both giggling away.

'You're funny, Mummy.'

'I should have been a comedian, shouldn't I, son?'

'You're not that funny!'

Suddenly a tall shadow looms. Tommi is in his jumper and boxers with much of his hair stuck to his head with sweat. He has red creases on his face from the cushion. Tasty.

'Ha ha ha! Daddy, you look ludicrous!'

That's Barney's new word. He uses it for everything.

Tommi takes up a mock fighter's stance to make Barney laugh.

I immediately thrust a large mug of strong coffee at him. He grabs it and drinks about half of it at once.

'You look gorgeous, Alice. Look at you!'

'Thank you. You want some breakfast?'

'Jesus no, I'm still full of biriyani.'

'Well, seeing as you slept in that jumper, you should probably get yourself into the shower.'

'Oh, thank you for pointing out I'm stinky.'

'I'm not saying that, I refuse to get close enough to find out.'

'Ha ha! Stinky Daddy.'

Tommi tickles our son then bounds upstairs with Barney running after him, trying as hard as possible to hit him on the bottom.

They do this all the time.

CHAPTER TWENTY-ONE

Did.

I pile empty bowls and cups into the dishwasher with last night's glasses and plates. Tommi said he'd be taking Barney to school again this morning. That's a world record. Twice in a week.

Is that it then? Us making another go of it?

Maybe that's how to do it. Just get back on the horse and make all the bad stuff go away. But Tommi still works with Em. Unless she suddenly leaves or gets sacked. How can I rest easy with him at that office? How can I ever go along to his work parties with her still there?

I can't help wondering how forgiving Tommi would be if he knew about Philo or Harry.

I stick some organic wholemeal into the toaster. It might, at least, drive the taste of doubt and shame from my mouth. And it'll make a change from alcohol. A text zings into my phone. It's from Suze.

Hey there amigo. Hope the sparks are flying again. Love to you both, S x

Suze is great but she just doesn't get it like Smithy does. Suddenly I feel like weeping. I pour another coffee.

CHAPTER TWENTY TWO

Harry's gone. And I have no idea where.

I got the shock of my life this morning when I arrived at work and saw Mr Glamour himself, Melissa's dad, standing at the water cooler. He was in a pale blue suit that looked fantastic in a *Charlie's Angels* kind of way, together with his silver fox hair and perma-tan. His teeth seemed even whiter than usual. Strangely he seemed to waiting for me. I'm so glad I got in ten minutes early. Being late with him there would have been rather embarrassing. Belle, of course, was already in.

She was chuntering on about some rubbish or other but when he saw me, he did a slight double take and said, 'Excuse me a moment, erm - '

'Belle!'

'Belle! Of course. A lovely name. Well, Belle, I need to speak to Alice here, if you don't mind. In private.'

Her mouth tightened into a little line and her eyes blazed like metal-rimmed flame throwers in my direction. She hates being kept out of the loop.

'Hello Alice.'

'Hello Mr. Benham. This is a nice surprise.'

CHAPTER TWENTY TWO

'Is it? Thank you. Same to you. Can I have a word in Harry's office please?'

'Of course.'

I followed him in, totally confused as this had never happened before. My mind began to whirr.

Oh my god, maybe the company is about to be unceremoniously shut down, here and now, by the big boss. But why would he just be telling me? Is he going to sack me? Where the hell is Harry?

Mr Benham closed the door and cleared his throat.

'So. I wanted to speak to you on your own because Harry tells me you are the most competent person in the office.'

'Oh, does he? The fool!'

I don't know why I said that. Thankfully he laughed.

'Ha. Yes. And he's... ah... had to go away. For a week.'

'Is he okay? He never said anything.'

'Yes, he's fine. Well, maybe a little stressed. Because of his stress, I told him to take some time off. Have a holiday. This place hasn't got too much on right now, so I wondered if you could hold the fort. Kind of act as manager until he comes back?'

'Really?'

'Yes. He said you saved his bacon when Hassan upped sticks and disappeared, so you clearly know what you're doing. I just need reassurance that everyone knows what they're doing until he comes back?'

There seemed to be a bit of an upward inflection on 'comes back', like there was a chance Harry wouldn't return. I felt a sick weight in the pit of my stomach. And not just because of last night's curry.

'Right. Well, of course. It won't be a problem. But what

should I tell the staff?'

'Oh. Just say there's been a family emergency and he'll be back next Monday.'

I think he just told me that I'm boss for the week. I'm almost sure that's what he just said.

'I'm sure I can manage that.'

He smiles his shiny all-American-looking smile.

'Glad to hear it. I've got to fly off to Milan in an hour so please call me if you have any problems.'

He handed me a card with his number on it.

'Of course.'

'Great. Well, enjoy having your own office. If I don't hear from you I'll call on Friday just to make sure all is well.'

'Fine.'

He moved to the door. Before opening it, he turned back.

'By the way, Alice - '

'Yes?'

'You look different. Have you had some work done?'

I didn't know whether to thump him or swoon.

'No. I just cheered up.'

'I like it.'

Cheeky twat.

I have Harry's number. I've been in his office for the last two hours wondering if I should text him. The whole thing seems a little strange. Mr Benham was so vague. If a family member has died or is ill, why not just say that? Why would Harry be having a holiday? God forbid that it's something to do with what happened between us.

I slump in my chair. At that moment Elen comes in without knocking. She's very excited that I'm in Harry's office. And seeing as she's my assistant and I'm training her, it seems logical to her that she should work in here too. I don't mind, because I like her and the others are happy enough to get on with their work in their usual spaces. Only Belle seems infuriated. She keeps walking past and glaring in. Or she did until I tilted the blind upwards so I didn't have to see her beaky face.

'Alice, you look great behind that desk.'

She's brought me a peppermint tea. I'm trying to have at least one hour in the day when I'm not guzzling caffeine. She herself has Diet Pepsi. She sits opposite me.

'Not much going on today.'

'I know. Which is why I've decided I'm leaving early. I'm perfectly entitled to sod off when I want now that I'm the boss.'

She high-fives me.

'Where you off?'

'Just family stuff.'

'How'd it go with Tommi last night?'

'Fine.'

'Fine? Didn't you fall into his arms and stay up all night, energetically reacquainting yourselves?'

'Nope.'

'Good. I wouldn't have had him back.'

'In fifteen years you'll think differently. Anyway, he's not "back" back. Not yet. He's got to prove himself.'

'I don't like it. If you need to cheat there's something wrong at home. In Tommi's case, he's wrong at home.'

'Elen!'

'When you came out to The Dog with us you had a ball. You were like this... this different person. I wish you'd come out again. At least it would shut Philo up. He asked for your number the other day, you know. He was jamming round

Noah's and he kept talking about you.'

Oh God. I assume a look of shock.

'Did he? Goodness, he's far too young for me.'

'I know he is, but it didn't stop him. Should I?'

'What?'

'Give him your number? Though I have to warn you, he's very bad. He has three girls wrapped around his finger at the moment. That's what Noah says.'

I shudder slightly. A competitive little imp inside me wonders if he'd drop all three of them if I showed any interest. I squash the imp.

'Don't you dare give my number to that boy. He might be handsome but I have enough problems.'

'What problems?'

'It's just a turn of phrase. I mean I have enough going on with Tommi and Barney, without the unwanted attentions of a sexy child.'

'So, you admit he's sexy?'

'I'm not blind.'

'You dirty old woman.'

She has no idea. Neither does my mum, who called last night and seemed over the moon to hear Tommi in the background, shouting hello.

'That's me. I'm filthy.'

'So's my Noah. Last night he –'

I put my hands over my ears and begin to, 'La-la-la-la,' loudly. When her mouth stops moving I take away my hands.

'Elen, I'm very pleased for you and all, but I can do without the ins and outs.'

'I *love* the ins and outs.'

So do I, but I'm not telling her that.

CHAPTER TWENTY THREE

Barney's face turns to sunshine when I show up outside his classroom. Pure, bright happiness. And suddenly the misty afternoon is summer. Or that's how it feels. Schmaltzy maybe, but perfectly true. When the door opens he flies out, forgetting his schoolboy cool, and grabs me around the waist.

'Mummy, what are you doing here? This is really good news.'

How can I not be disarmed?

'We have an ice-cream parlour to visit, have we not?'

'Really?'

'Really.'

I pick him up and kiss him on his boy-flavoured face. I know picking your own child up from school isn't a Nobel Prize-winning act but it feels quite fabulous right now. He remembers that it is not good school etiquette to be picked up and kissed by your mum, and he wriggles himself back to the ground. He does however take my hand.

'Let's *go!*'

Other children and mothers are milling all over the schoolyard. As I begin to guide us towards the gate, I nod at a few faces I recognise. One lady, a nice smiley one in wellies and a long floral skirt who has twin girls in Barney's class, stops me on the way.

'Are you coming to parents' drinks tomorrow?'

'Oh. I didn't know…'

'It was in a letter in their book bags last week. Don't worry, I always forget to look, too. Anyway, it's eight 'til closing at The Alex if you fancy. Most of the year are going, so there'll be a nice crowd. I don't get out much so I'm looking forward to it.'

'Mummy, come on. I want peanut butter and poo ice-cream!'

Barney is pulling my arm. If I don't move soon he'll yank it out of its socket.

'Thank you for telling me, erm…'

'Caroline.'

'Caroline, of course, I'm so sorry. I'm at work so much I forget everyone's name.'

'Don't worry. Hope you can make it!'

I give her a wave as Barney drags me off. He is burbling with excitement. He keeps up a monologue about dinosaurs for the whole fifteen-minute walk. I nod and 'oh' and 'ah' but really he's talking because he's happy so my interjections aren't required.

As I walk, I realise that many of the mums and dads will know Marina, our childminder, much better than they know me. She probably stops and chats with them, knows the other kids in Barney's class, maybe hears the titbits of school gossip. I usually drop him off in the mornings but I'm in too much of a hurry for more than a perfunctory 'hello' to the other parents. I need to make more of an effort. I couldn't make any of the school socials last year. I say couldn't. Didn't want to. Too tired, too wrapped up in work and my own woes. Tomorrow I will make an effort. Tomorrow I will be a proper participant

CHAPTER TWENTY THREE

in the school social calendar.

The ice-cream parlour is a nice, clean-looking café. I'm still a little shaky in the tummy after last night's blow out but I chance a fresh strawberry sorbet, which, it turns out, is beautiful. Next time, I want the coconut and the Turkish delight. They look amazing. Barney spoons his into his mouth in almost complete silence. When he's enjoying something he goes into a trance. It's hilarious to watch him, eyes glazed over, spoon connecting with mouth, connecting with icy dessert, connecting with mouth again. Sometimes I can't believe how perfect he is. How long his limbs are getting. How cheeky his grey eyes are. Eyes just like his dad's. This place is rammed with parents who look to be enjoying the ice creams as much as the kids are. I have no interest in other people's rowdy kids and some in here are spoilt little shits, I can see it. But others, as I scan the room, are polite, well-behaved small people, having conversations with their mums and dads and savouring their treats.

Suddenly, Barney looks up at me, all serious.

'Mummy, thank you for bringing me here. This is the best ice cream in England. Definitely.'

He has ice cream on his nose and running down his chin. I wipe him with a serviette.

'Also I'm glad to see you because I have an announcement to make'

'Oh goodness, have you? What's your announcement?'

'I have a wobbly tooth. Look!'

He wobbles his front tooth on the top. I can't help laughing. My boy is growing up. I ruffle his hair across the table. He pretends to purr. He's always wanted a cat.

Suddenly I feel emotional. I want more of this. I may not

be the world's best mum, but I want to pick my boy up from school sometimes. I don't think that's too much ask. When you're five, a little thing can make a day the best day of your life so far. I feel like I'm not giving him enough 'best days'.

'Mummy, can I watch a spooky film when we get home, please?'

'Why not.'

'*Whoaaaaa*. This is ludicrous. Will you watch it with me?'

'I might.'

'Woohoo!'

And that's it. Best day of his life. Until the next one.

CHAPTER TWENTY-FOUR

The Alex is rammed. Bloody typical, they're having a social for the whole year, that's three classes worth of parents, but they've chosen a pub that's popular anyway, so it's heaving. Nice one, class reps. I didn't want to dress up too much and it's pretty freezing outside tonight, so I put on some nice knee-high boots I got in a sale yesterday with a black denim mini skirt, black thick tights and a bright red top with long sleeves. I haven't told Tommi about the emergency card yet. I'll just have to try to pay bits off on the sly. I'm going to boil in my own juices in here. Great. I spot a bunch of mums sitting at a table a few feet away. One of them with trendy glasses, wearing some kind of kaftan, waves at me. Another one of them, a tiny little woman with short, mousy 'mum' hair, is talking rather loudly about her daughter's achievements at ballet class. I need a drink before I get into this.

As I was leaving tonight, five minutes after tucking Barney up and doing our little 'bonne nuit' routine, Tommi followed me to the door and thanked me for going without him. We could have got a sitter but he hates the whole school socialising thing. In the end, many more mums than dads come to these gatherings so it wasn't like I was disappointed he wouldn't come. No, we have our 'going out' night planned for Friday when my mum is babysitting. Our first night out together since the 'incident' with Em. Just to test the water, of course. But anyway, after thanking me, he planted a kiss on my lips and allowed his hand to stray down the zip on the side of my top and onto my backside. It hit me then that I might have to attempt some intimacy very soon.

I'm nervous about it, but if we're going to try to make things work I'm going to have to do it sometime. Maybe it would be best to get vaguely well oiled, go home at a reasonable hour and get it over with. That sounds bad, but the first time is always going to be weird. Someone once told me that in a long relationship, sex becomes a balm. A healing thing. Even when you don't think you feel like it, you should consider it anyway. Maybe breaking that barrier tonight will help everything go back to normal. Even if his constant messing with the TV channels drives me insane; even if he really wound me up by coming home tonight with only ten minutes to spare when he knew I was going out.

The bar is crowded. I move to the end to see if I can get served more quickly. As I do, a mum appears by my side. She's a class rep called Debbie. I know this because Debbie sends at least three emails a day to all of us parents, of which I read very few. And when I drop Barney in the mornings she's usually buzzing around, speaking authoritatively about class business and being over-familiar with harried mums and dads. She has a boy in our class called Edward. He's gorgeous to look at but whines a lot (that's what Barney says, anyway). She seems to consider herself Queen of the Reps. She's welcome to her title.

Debbie has small features, like a ferret, and a mass of curly, high-maintenance hair. She looks like an 1990s throwback, always tries too hard when she's accessorising, and has an extremely high voice. My heart sinks when I see her. She reminds me of Belle because she always seems to be poking about, trying to get into people's business. When she puts her hand on my arm it gets worse. It means she's going to speak to me. Blast.

'Hiya, Alice. How are you?'

'I'm fine thanks. A bit hot.'

She speaks with the kind of voice I'd expect a teapot to have.

'Yes, it's popular here, isn't it?'

'It is.'

I turn and order a glass of Prosecco. She stays put as the bar girl goes to get it.

'So, I was hoping to speak to you about Barney.'

'What about Barney?'

'Well. It's a bit delicate. I mean, it's nobody's business what happens behind closed doors.'

Damn right it isn't. I already don't like where this is going. I pay for my drink.

'But it has to be said, he hasn't seemed himself recently. A bit impatient, snappy even. Apparently he told Edward to "stop being a pain in the arse" last week.'

She whispers 'arse' like it's the most scandalous word possible.

'I mean, that's not acceptable language at any age, let alone five. Plus he's been a little quiet. Sometimes he doesn't reply when I say hello to him in the morning, which isn't like him at all.'

'Perhaps you just get on his nerves as much your son does' is what I think, but the blood is rushing to my head too quickly for me to reply. I just let her carry on.

'What I was wondering is, is he getting enough organic produce? Processed stuff can have such a bad effect on their metabolisms and make them grouchy, can't it? Otherwise, is everything okay at home? Parental relationships can really impact on the kids. You can talk to me about anything you like, you know. I mean, me and Andrew have a strict policy of not arguing in front of Isabella and Edw – '

I have to stop this, right now.

'Barney eats very well, thank you, Debbie. I cook and freeze everything from scratch. Just to put your mind at rest, when I home-make the sauce for his wholewheat pasta it always contains greens, usually kale. As for his 'grouchiness' he's just a normal five-year-old who gets the same moods as other kids. In fact, my friend's four-year-old daughter told her grandma to fuck off recently because she didn't want to eat her carrots.'

Debbie's mouth makes a small 'o' as the f-bomb is dropped. And I have actually never cooked kale in my life.

'She'd heard a young man saying it on the bus and was extremely impressed. And as for the offer of a chat about parenting, that's lovely of you, but if there really was a problem at home, which there isn't, I think I'd probably be more inclined to chat to a friend about it, to be honest.'

The glint in her eye is unreadable. I doubt it's possible to embarrass her so she's either pissed off I wouldn't spill, or feeling murderous that I'm not her 'friend'.

'Okay, Alice. Enjoy your evening.'

As she moves off, I hear a man laugh and turning to my right, look straight into the amused face of 'Sexy Dad'.

'That told her.'

He has a northern accent and when he smiles I see a small chip in his tooth. The accent jars with his Italian looks. He has a very deep voice. Almost weirdly so. I'm shaking a bit. The talk of Barney and my relationship was too close to home. Stupid cow.

'Was I horrible?'

'You're kidding. That woman has been in my face since the start of term. She's relentless. Good on you. One sign of weakness and you'd have been her new project.'

'Why are people so nosy? That's why I hate these socials.'

'Me too. Let's hide.'

He pays for the pint of Guinness which has appeared in front of him and indicates two high stools at the bar that are surrounded by businessmen but not being used. I notice the bar girl turning a little pink when he smiles at her. It's probably that tooth; a handsome man with a cheeky-boy chip at the front is always going to be attractive.

Once we sit down, we are in the corner of the bar and thoroughly shielded by the men in suits who are talking about football. The least interesting thing I could ever think of talking about, apart from cricket, is football.

'Why has that appalling harpy been in your face all term then?'

'Because she's a busybody, because she's as nosy as my granny and because she probably fancies me.'

I almost squirt fizz through my nose.

'Is that so?'

'Of course. Why else would she fix on a bloke whose daughter isn't in her son's class? She's not my rep. But she keeps trying to find out if I'm single by asking about my wife. I'll bet her husband is a henpecked so-and-so. I'm telling her nothing. She can peck away.'

'But wouldn't it be easier to tell her the truth? Then she

might leave you alone.'

'*Oh*. Is that you pecking now?'

I can't work out if he's arrogant or just has a dry sense of humour. It's probably both.

'If I was going to "peck", I probably wouldn't choose a dad from school. Talk about gossip central.'

'Hm, interesting. You didn't jump in with "no, I'm married", you just wouldn't want anyone to know what you're up to.'

What a strange man.

He regards me for a moment, biting his extraordinarily well-shaped bottom lip.

'Being a bit too cocky, aren't I? Can I get you another?'

'I'm not sure. I might just go home.'

'Oh, come on. Don't leave me to face this alone. Have one more, while I finish this pint, then I'll go home as well.'

'Okay. A Prosecco, please.'

'Coming up.'

As he orders I study him. He's like a forty-odd year-old Al Pacino and only slightly taller. He's wearing a casual navy shirt with a leather jacket. It's soft and expensive-looking and much as I feel sorry for the animal that died to make it, it smells good. His whole look, complete with olive skin, Botticelli lips and chipped tooth, is 'expensive Italian rogue' and he pulls it off well. When my drink arrives he pushes it towards me.

'There you go. Alice.'

He laughs when he sees my surprise. A deep, throaty thing, it is.

'Don't panic. I heard Debbie call you, Alice. I'm Santo. It means saint.'

He puts out his hand and I have to shake it. Warm, dry and strong. His palms are soft. When he moves he smells of leather

CHAPTER TWENTY-FOUR

and something citrus. It's hard not to be aware of him, he's very 'present'.

'Why am I thinking you were named ironically?'

This time his laugh is surprised.

'You're funny.'

He sips his Guinness. I don't know how he manages to avoid a froth moustache.

'Now I'm going to let you into a little secret. I already knew who you were. Not your name, but I knew your little boy was Barney. My daughter told me. She plays with him sometimes. I think she's got a crush.'

'Oh, how sweet.'

'My Luisa.'

He says it with some pride. We parents just can't help it.

'Yes, he mentioned her. But I thought it was Louisa.'

'Most people do, I pronounce it like the Italians do. I'm pretentious like that. But, going back to you, here's the thing I need to ask. One day you were just another mum; nice face, tired looking, shuffling in at five to nine, looking at the ground and wrapped up in layers. Next thing out of nowhere, you're about a foot taller, you've got a waist and you're a knockout. Dads in the yard are literally landing face first on the tarmac. What happened? I'm curious.'

'Jesus. That's a bit melodramatic. I just bought some colourful clothes.'

'Bollocks.'

'What?'

'The clothes were the least of it. Your head was up, your hair was different, you started holding yourself like you owned the place. At the risk of sounding like a misogynist bastard, you looked like you suddenly found out you were hot stuff and wanted to flaunt it. And there's nothing sexier than confidence.'

'You don't mince your words, do you?'

'No. Tell it like it is. Always best.'

I sit and take this in. 'Sexy Dad' has been watching me. I like his voice and his mouth and just about everything else, but I don't plan to tell that like it is. Because I think he's a cocky twat. There's one thing I can be honest about though.

'My other half pissed me off. I decided to have a makeover to cheer myself up.'

'I see.'

He doesn't look surprised.

'That would explain a lot.'

'What would explain a lot?'

'Let me take a punt. Women sometimes lose their mojo when they have children. Get depressed, don't like themselves, get tired, don't want their husband near them. Next thing you know... the guy starts feeling pushed out. He cheats, or gets fancied by someone else, she finds out, thinks "fuck you" and suddenly gets her mojo back. Not always for him though.'

How the hell..?

'That's a bit presumptuous.'

'No, it's not. I've been there.'

'Oh?'

'My wife was paranoid after Luisa was born. Thought I was going to cheat on her. She took a while to lose the belly, she hated her breasts and she thought she looked ten years older. I liked her bigger but she wouldn't believe me. And the real problem? Work. She loved it. Felt she was nothing without her job, but also felt guilty for wanting to go to back, so she stayed home for three years and it nearly killed her. She hated how she looked, so she hated going out and she was terrified of me going out without her in case I found someone else. It's terrible having a confident, beautiful wife who suddenly has no sense of self-worth at all. Eventually, I told her, "Go back to work, you're insane." So she went. She was away for three months, only back on weekends.'

'Wow. What does she do?'

'Continuity on films and TV. She sits with a script and watches everything and makes sure that the actors say the same thing every time, that their hair's the same way, their glass has the same amount of water in it, blah de blee. It's a painstaking job but she loves it. And within weeks she was more her old self again. She was swimming at the hotel when she wasn't filming. The exercise was making her feel better. She still felt guilty for leaving Luisa, but we had Skype in the week and I stopped working and became Daddy Daycare.'

'What's your job?'

'I'm an electrician. They call us "sparks" on set. I met her on a shit film that never got released.'

'And? You got bored and cheated?'

'No darlin', she did.'

I wasn't expecting that.

'She did.'

'Of course she did. She got her sense of worth back by having sex with a besotted new bloke. Somewhere in her head it was my fault she lost her confidence. Women like me a lot, you see.'

I look down at the floor so I don't catch his eye. The cocky sod.

'When she felt bad about herself she hated women liking me. Relationships are hard. Having a baby can be the biggest bomb in any relationship. Insurmountable, sometimes.'

Who'd have thought it? 'Sexy Dad' being a relationship sage.

'Did you split up?'

He shows me that chipped tooth again when he smiles.

'Nope. Well, not for long. When she got back from the job I knew something was up. Someone kept ringing her and she'd leave the room to speak. Then out of nowhere she got a new phone and changed her number. Turned out this bloke wanted things to continue and she realised she wanted us. Me and Luisa. When she told me, I only wanted to know two things. Did she love him and did she use condoms? She said a big no to the first one and a definite yes to the second one, thank God. That would have been a deal breaker for me. So disrespectful.'

'And you stayed with her?'

'Yup. Almost, but not entirely, as it was before.'

He smiles again. I wonder if he means what I think he means.

'I won't leave her, she's my wife. But she works away a lot, while I stay here. Like you said, Santo by name, not by nature.'

'Bloody hell. Mine didn't cheat that badly. Just a drunken fumble.'

'I see. But the big question is, what did you do when you found out he fumbled? Apart from wreaking havoc among the dads?'

I can't help a laugh.

'I kicked him.'

He snorts.

'Good start. Fancy a liqueur?'

My glass is empty. So is his. Why not? I am utterly amused when he gets us both a large amaretto on ice. Such a sweet drink for such a macho-looking bloke.

'Come on then. Did you stay with him, your husband?'

CHAPTER TWENTY-FOUR

'Not husband, partner.'

Despite having what seems to be a Sheffield accent, he mutters something in Italian and shakes his head.

'Legally it is ridiculous not to be married if you have children together.'

'I don't care about legality. Marriage isn't for everyone. And now I'm glad we're not married.'

'Right, so you split up?'

'No. Well, he stayed with some friends for a while but two nights ago he moved back in.'

'So you're together again.'

'Not quite.'

Unexpectedly he angles his body towards me, one knee suddenly against mine and looks me full in the face.

'If you're not ready to have him in your bed, why is he back?'

I begin to ramble.

'He... Well, I will but... Anyway... that's quite a personal thing... because... Well, it's only sex.'

'Only sex? Only sex? You're telling me you're not a passionate woman? If you don't want sex with him, maybe you should have left him at his friend's house. I may have my secrets but I still fancy my wife.'

I'm tempted to slap him. I don't like him talking about Tommi that way. Partly because it makes me feel disloyal and partly because he's right.

CHAPTER TWENTY-FIVE

As I'm coming out of the pub loo I check my watch. It's hardly ten o'clock. For some ridiculous reason I've accepted a lift home from Santo. I hope Tommi doesn't see me getting out of his car. I mean, it's another parent so it should be fine, but it's a bloke, a bloke who's over the drink driving limit actually and to be frank, Santo doesn't look like your average school dad.

As I'm heading for the door I see the smiley mum, who invited me – Caroline wasn't it? – talking to a tall, very skinny, balding man. I wonder if it's her husband. She's wearing a multi-coloured cardigan and is being rather effusive with her hand gestures. I think she may be drunk. I hope she doesn't spot me as I'll have to go over there and I want to leave. I put my head down and aim for the exit. Luckily I make it outside without incident, but am pulled up short by the temperature drop. It's so cold. Jesus, it's gone to sub-zero in a couple of hours. I see a parked car with its headlamps on, not far away, and rush towards it. I can't tell what colour it is but it's big and when I get in it's already warming up from the full-blast heating.

As I put on my seatbelt, the back of my hand grazes Santo's, on the gearstick. Neither of us says anything but this sudden close proximity in the dark of the car, without anyone else around, is a little overwhelming. At least for me it is. Our conversation was a bit full on for someone I've never spoken to before. I don't know this perplexing man at all, but he's basically just admitted he's a married player. Appallingly I don't give a hoot. My main line of thought is this: if I'm supposed to go home and seduce or at least allow myself to be seduced by my long-term partner tonight, why am I having to try so hard not to fantasise about kissing the man sitting next to me in this car?

'I live just off Dexter Road. Do you know it?'

'I know it.'

He pulls off fast and the wrong way.

'Where are you going?'

'Just a little place I know.'

I think I must look scared because he smiles.

'Five minutes. Don't worry.'

'I don't want to be kidnapped, Santo.'

He stops the car. Right in the middle of the road. I glance out of the back window; luckily there's no-one behind us.

'I can cut down Durham Street right there and have you home in a few minutes. Or you can trust me and let me have a few more minutes of your time, then drive you home. What do you think?'

As we're sitting, a car comes up behind us. I see the headlights in the rear-view mirror. After several seconds it beeps its horn. I should go home. My behaviour is getting 'ludicrous', as Barney would say. I look at Santo who is looking back, quite levelly, taking absolutely no notice of the pissed-off driver behind who is beeping again.

'Okay. Detour. Short detour.'

'Good.'

He takes off down the street and shoots a right then a left. Soon I spot the local woods. There's a park in there and many entrances. One road to the park is off the street where Barney went to nursery. I've seen it many times but have never driven down it. When we turn into it, I realise that it's very short, comprising of a little row of cottages and a small community centre, ending in the locked park gate. Down the side of the community centre, there's a tiny alleyway. Santo drives us through it and into a small car park with railing down the side of it, right next to the woods. He parks the car close to the building, facing the railings and trees. The back door and windows of the building have metal shutters. He cuts the engine. As the car stops, my heart speeds up a little. Plays a mini samba.

'My daughter used to come here when she was tiny. When I picked her up on dark evenings, I noticed the security camera and lights were set quite far out into the car park. As long as you drive in close to the wall and back out the same way, the light doesn't come on and the camera is focused another three or so feet that way.'

I have a peek and can see he's right.

'How did you know they hadn't moved it?'

'I didn't. Thought I'd risk it.'

There's a loaded silence. I don't know why I'm here, apart from maybe the obvious.

'You've not brought me here to kill me, have you?'

'Not quite.'

'So what are we doing here?'

'Talk. Away from a bar full of annoying people.'

CHAPTER TWENTY-FIVE

'Strange place for a chat.'

'I had to improvise.'

'Improvise or return to your "usual" haunt?'

'Is that you pecking again?'

He's so sure of himself. I'm not used to it. He just seems to say whatever takes his fancy.

'No.'

'You obviously think I'm some sort of playboy, but I'm not.'

'But you said - '

'I said I'm not a saint. No-one is. I've wandered about the park at night but haven't been here before. Are you nervous?'

Truth or bluff? I'm terrified.

'Yes.'

'Why?'

'I'm in a car with a stranger in the dark. No-one knows where I am and I don't know why I agreed to come here.'

'You don't?'

'No.'

'I think you do.'

'Am I wrong in thinking you're a bit arrogant?'

'No. I pretty much believe I'm God's gift. But that's not what this is about. Can I ask you something?'

'If you must.'

'If life wasn't full of fucking rules, right now, what would you do?'

'Oh, come on, Mr Slick.'

'Tell the truth.'

He isn't touching me. He isn't being creepy. He is just looking at me.

'Nothing I could do in a car.'

'Oh really?'

'Really.'

He reaches under his seat, pushes a lever and suddenly moves back a couple of feet.

'Roomy car, Alice.'

'Oh.'

Suddenly I catch my breath as he scoots close, dips his hand under my chair and moves that back too.

He laughs. This man doesn't give a shit, he just does what he pleases. I start to panic and any old rubbish tumbles out of my blundering mouth.

'I don't even know if Tommi had full sex with that idiot in his office. I think I need to get home. I promised myself that I'd be good...'

'Shhhh. No talk of him. What a passion killer. If you wanted him, you'd be home right now. Fact.'

'Please don't say that. It makes me feel shit.'

'I suspect you spend your life feeling shit anyway.'

'Everyone spends their life feeling shit.'

'Not me. How about you stop feeling shit and kiss me?'

'What?'

'I'm not kissing you. You want to kiss me, you come over here.'

'Oh my God. What is your problem?'

'At the moment, you are. I saw you in the playground the other day and got such a major erection I didn't know if I'd be able to walk to my car.'

He terrifies me so much.

'You are so out of order.'

'What's wrong with wanting you? You can say no. I'll drop you home, go back to my house and pleasure myself in the shower. And your name will be on my lips while I do it.'

CHAPTER TWENTY-FIVE

I can't help staring at his mouth when he says this. Is that the plan? Make me look at his mouth? Part of me wonders how many women he's said this to. Another part of me is molten lava.

'I can't. Apart from anything else, I'd be risking my health.'

'Well, that's nice, isn't it? But actually, very sensible. I commend you.'

He reaches into the inside pocket of his jacket, opens a small wallet and takes out a condom. He places it on the dashboard.

'Now what?'

'Why are you carrying a condom?'

'I always have one on me. It's probably a year old, but it's fine.'

'You've got an answer for everything.'

'You've got an argument for everything.'

'Is your wife at home?'

'No. But thanks for bringing her up. My wife is away on a job in Cyprus. It's been a long one. But this weekend she's back and it's my turn.'

'Meaning?'

'Meaning she'll be back and I'll start my job on Monday. For five months. I'll be back at night to see Luisa, but you will have the pleasure of my wife doing the school run. She says she's happy to do half a year of childcare but I very much doubt it. She'll be demented within a week and her mum will have to take over. Will you miss me?'

'Christ, you're so vain.'

'I'll miss you, sexy mama.'

'Stop it!'

'Giving me hard-ons in the playground. Marching about in your red shoes…'

He turns towards me, leans against his door and opens his arms.

'Free pass tonight. You won't even have to see me at school. You can pretend it was all a wonderful dream.'

Why am I so turned on by this dick-head?

Embarrassingly, I find myself clambering onto his lap. I put my back to his window and he puts his right arm lightly around my shoulder.

'Well hello, sexy mama.'

I still can't get over that improbably deep voice. And this close, his lips are even more beautiful. I can feel the heat of his legs through my skirt and tights. Because it's dark, his face is silhouetted in moonlight. He looks like a sculpture.

'Too warm in here for that coat, don't you think?'

I swallow before I reply.

'Far too warm.'

I slip my coat awkwardly over my shoulders and he helps manoeuvre it off and push it into the foot well. What I'm doing has no excuse, I don't even know if I like this man. I am now a true slut. This thought does not turn me off. Instead, I take his face in my hands and kiss him hard. His reaction is unhurried but confident, as it's been all night. His left hand insinuates itself into my waistband and stays there, as his hot tongue entwines with mine. I don't know what it is about this situation but I am so turned on I am shaking. My tongue seeks out his chipped tooth and finding the pointy roughness of it gives me great satisfaction. His hands aren't everywhere and he is simply kissing me back but, suddenly, all I want is to do is shag him into next week. I twist my body as I kiss him and reach down the side of his seat. I locate a little lever and the back of his chair lowers, giving us more room. As it moves he

CHAPTER TWENTY-FIVE

laughs.

'Jesus, am I about to be raped?'

'Maybe.'

He struggles out of his jacket then lays back again, with me still perched on his lap, my feet stretching over to the passenger seat.

I kiss him harder and feel the fire ignite even more when his hand moves to a zip on my top.

'What do we have here, then?'

He pulls the zip upwards. It's a fashion statement rather than something that's needed, in fact there's a zip on each side, up my ribcage; but it doesn't lessen the thrill as he inches it up and the air reaches my skin. So that he can get to the other zip, I shift position and straddle him. It's a tight squeeze and my skirt isn't very stretchy so I hitch it up around my hips. Straddling his jeans in tights with built-in knickers, those ones that are about two hundred denier, makes it hard to feel anything, so I reach down to his fly and feel the gratifying hardness beneath the denim with my hand. That's when he emits a groan and mutters again in Italian. This time he unzips my other zip fast and grips my back.

'Are you going to take this off for me?'

I don't need asking twice. I bend forward and awkwardly slip it over my head. In the cooling car I feel my nipples become hard. I am wearing the last of my clean bras. It is white with little cherries printed on it. I wonder if it's too girly or silly, but from the way he is looking at me I don't think it is.

As I kiss him again, he whispers, 'Take that off, too.'

And like the rampant hussy I've become, I loosen the catch and lower it from my shoulders, exposing the breasts I've been so ashamed of since they got so big. But big doesn't seem to be a problem for Santo. His first reaction in to gasp

'Jesus.'

He moves his hands to my bottom and pulls me up his body so his mouth can take in an erect nipple and bite, almost painfully, into the pink flesh. I grip the headrest of the seat as he does the same to the other then kisses, bites and caresses at will. After a while I pull back and begin to unbutton his shirt, trying not to bang my head on the ceiling. He has dark chest hair. When he tries to help me undo his shirt I push his hands away, wanting to unveil him myself, then he levers himself up the seat so I can undo his belt and zip.

He's right about the car being roomy. I don't think we could do this in a Mini.

His belly also has dark hair and when I reach inside his jeans I find a very hard, very willing cock that seems to bend slightly to the left. I grip it firmly just to hear him groan. With my other hand I delve in and grip his bare and surprisingly pert behind. With a bit of difficulty he levers down his jeans, with me still straddling him, then kicks them off. I wonder how the hell I can get off my tights, skirt, and boots without doing myself an injury.

I lean into him, my bare breasts against his skin and kiss him, stroking his cock with my hand, then find myself biting his shoulder as he solves my problem by reaching down, pulling my skirt up even further and ripping the gusset of my tights in half. Suddenly I feel the cool air against my damp, hot self and without a word he slips his fingers inside me and bites my skin as I gasp into his hair. Now I am almost naked in a car with an Italian northerner and his hand is sending an electric Morse code through my nerves.

It's then that I have one of those moments that I usually only have in dreams. When I don't care anymore and I just want what I want and nothing will stop me. I twist as far as possible, reach to the dashboard and grab the condom. In what seems like seconds it is open and I have slid it onto his erection.

'Oh God.'

His eyes half close as I lower myself onto him. I gasp in shock as I fill up with someone who isn't Tommi, fill up and begin to move against this other man, one knee chafing against the door, the other knocking the gearstick. This man who is pulling me down hard on him again and again. This man who is running his nails down my back and whispering things in another language. I love the feel of the hair on his stocky, strong body and how his hands wander where they will, grabbing and stroking me. With another manipulation of the chair he flattens it as much as possible so that it rests against the back seat. Then, wriggling and fighting his way round, he manages to wrestle me over so that he's on top and I'm way up towards the back seat and I'm wrapping my boots deliciously around his ribcage as he pushes himself deeper and deeper inside me. It takes a ridiculously short time before I'm feeling that fluttering in my pelvis. A flutter that turns into waves of helpless spasms. Just as I'm disappearing into the abyss, I see Santo's face contort with pleasure and hear him gasp his appreciation. Fucking Santo is like coming to the end of a sparring match and winning.

And thus ends my first ever, fully realised, one-night stand.

CHAPTER TWENTY SIX

Anybody in the world who wears crotchless knickers must be insane or just doesn't do it on a cold night, in a short skirt, while they're damp from illicit sex. Because that's what I, in effect, am doing right now as I walk along my freezing street. Santo dropped me off at the corner; there was no way he could drop me at my door. I'm a little late and have to make it look like I caught the bus.

Tonight he made it very clear that he is not going to leave his wife, that he is going away to work on Monday and that he is not always a 'good boy'. He dropped these facts like careless lumps of sugar in coffee. I am under no illusion about him and that is probably why I let go like I did. And now, he is already being consigned to the 'one-off' box in the back of my brain. His cockiness was sexy for a brief encounter. More than that and I would punch his lights out. I have never ever behaved like this in my life. What the bloody hell?

And now I have to come up with a plan. Because I have to get into the house and have a wash and throw away my ripped tights before Tommi notices anything. Plus I need to think. Because if I can disrespect my other half enough to fuck someone else while I'm supposed to be having sex with him,

CHAPTER TWENTY SIX

then there is something seriously wrong.

About ten houses from my front door though, I slow my steps. Many of the houses on our street contain children, and a lot of them at twenty to midnight are already dark for the night. Very rarely do we see 'strangers' wandering around. But I can see someone in the road up ahead, standing stock still, and it gives me the creeps. I step away from the streetlight so they can't see me. It's someone in a parka with the hood up. These days, 'hoods' are associated with muggings and stabbings and this, at the very least, looks like a mad bloke. Just standing there in his jeans and trainers and hoodie, staring at - I creep closer... Our house.

Oh Christ. There's a weirdo watching our upstairs window. How will I get past without him seeing me? I don't know what to do. If I ring Tommi will the crazy man hear me? I take out my phone, duck behind a low wall and call Tommi's number. It's switched off. Shit.

I stand again and reach into my bag, taking out my pen. It's silver with my name engraved on it. My parents got it for me with a silver pencil for Christmas. I thought it was a strange gift at the time, but now I realise this pen might save me if I have to take drastic measures and use it as a stabbing weapon.

I also take out my keys and, keeping close to the walls and hedges, advance forwards. Within three doors of my house the 'hoodie' hasn't moved an inch and I begin to consider doubling back and calling the police. Then, horribly, the pen in my hand hits against the buckle on my bag and makes a clanking sound. It's probably not loud but to me it sounds like a giant gong. And the hoodie hears it. He wheels round and looks straight at me. I prepare to attack with my pen, then stop dead.

I was right about one thing, it's definitely a lunatic. But it's not a man. It's Rabbit Face. As she turns her hood moves and in the lamplight I see her tears. She is standing outside out house blubbing. What the hell?

'What are you doing?'

'I... I'm... ask him!'

She breaks into a run down the street. I think about running after her but it's bloody baltic out here. And then a movement catches my eye. The spare room blinds twitch. I see a slight change in the corner of the window pane, soft blue light then darkness again. Tommi's there. He's hiding!

When I get in the house the lights are out. And the little box for the doorbell is open with the batteries taken out. I remove my boots and go upstairs. There isn't a sound. I check on Barney and he is fast asleep with a pillow on his head. He always puts a pillow on his head and it always freaks me out. But he's breathing and fine and smells like my usual musty, warm little boy. I kiss his sweaty head then make my way to my room. Head spinning, I drag off my tights and shove them into the bin, then put on my pyjama bottoms, a big jumper and my slippers. One little walk up the street and my hands and feet are like ice. Tommi is lying on the bed in the spare room with the TV on very quietly, seemingly fast asleep. I switch on the lights.

'Knock it off, Tommi. I saw you looking out of the window.

He doesn't move.

'Tommi! I'm not an imbecile.'

He opens one eye. It is rather red. He sits up.

'Sorry. I had a bottle of wine and dozed off.'

'Oh, did you? So you didn't know that your girlfriend was waiting outside the house, weeping like a total basket case?'

His attempt at an innocent face is comic.

CHAPTER TWENTY SIX

'Was she?'

'Of course she was. You've taken the batteries out of the doorbell. She must have been there a while.'

He grabs a half-finished glass of red wine from the bedside table and scratches his head like an aggravated monkey.

'She was here ages, Al. It was a nightmare.'

'Come downstairs.'

He follows me obediently.

I flick on the heating and pour myself a drink. He sits in the armchair so I have to sit on the sofa. This irritates me even more than usual.

'What's going on?'

He sighs the sigh of an old man.

'She won't take no for an answer. That's what.'

'But she's at work all day with you. Haven't you made it clear already?'

'Of course, but it's not enough. She's not so bad at work because I'm in her sight. But she says she gets upset thinking of me at night and needs to see me.'

I'm not buying this.

'What? But even if you were single, and you'd copped off with her at a party, you'd be entitled to tell her you don't want anything else. People break up all of the time. Have you told her?'

'I've told her everything 'til I'm blue in the face, but it makes no difference.'

'You need to get her sacked, then.'

'What?'

'You can't work with someone that crazy.'

Suddenly he looks worried.

'I can't do that.'

'Why not?'

'It would be her word against mine. And after what happened in the car, they could sack me.'

'Why?'

'Well, she wouldn't be this obsessed if I hadn't led her on.'

Aha. Bingo.

He leans his forehead into his hands.

'I'm so sorry, Al. She woke up Barney by ringing the bell. I told her through the letterbox to go away, but she wouldn't. Then she stopped knocking but I had to turn off my phone so I didn't get any more calls.'

I can't help feeling a little introspective here. Even though I'm now positive he must have done more with Em than he says he has, how can I possibly give him trouble for it? I suspect he's been a massive dick-head but what I've done is much worse than what he's done. I have wittingly been intimate with three men, one of them full intercourse, two of them married. I am much worse than Em. I am the kind of woman that other women despise. Em is in love with Tommi, which means she's done whatever she's done because she wants a proper relationship with him, and he obviously told her things weren't great for us at home. I now feel a bit sorry for her. A bit. But I can't have Barney being disturbed because of her madness.

'Has she gone?'

He is such a wuss.

'Yes, she ran for it.'

'Can't I sleep in your... our room, tonight? Having you next to me would be nice.'

I don't want him in my bed.

'Tommi - '

CHAPTER TWENTY SIX

He gives me the doggiest of puppy eyes. I have no idea how to say no. It's like Santo said, if I don't want him in my bed, why have I allowed him home? I wish he wasn't home. What a mess.

The thought of Santo brings me up short. I feel grubby. I need to wash.

'Look, I got so cold coming home; I'm going to have a nice hot bath. If you want to go into our room that's fine, but no funny business, okay?'

'Thank you.'

He jumps out of the seat and gets on the sofa next to me. He hugs me around the waist and puts his head on my lap, something he often did, before our little 'break'.

'I don't blame you being pissed off. I just wish we could be back to normal again.'

'I'm not sure what normal is any more Tommi.'

'Hm.'

He's already nodding off. When I go to the kitchen to wash out my glass I see a finished bottle of red plus another that's been half quaffed. Wow. He really went for it tonight.

When I'm in the en-suite the irony doesn't escape me, that I'm back from a night out, having had an illicit encounter in a car, and I'm now having a bath while my 'partner' sleeps. But I'm not drunk. Which means I'm the biggest baddie.

As I'm drying myself, I hear Tommi stumble into the bedroom and flop down on the bed. When I peep round the door, he's on top of the bedcovers in a T-shirt and boxers looking like the world's biggest toddler. So far, in the few days he's been back, I've not been able to shake the feeling of a relative stranger being here for a visit. Now, looking at him, I feel slight affection and nothing else for this big sleeping boy.

And it hits me, along with a wave of mild panic, that I could happily live the rest of my life without ever having sex with him again. That is definitely not good. I've been trying so hard to avoid thinking how splitting up would traumatise our son. But how can I change how I feel? Maybe I'm having a midlife crisis?

As I prepare to dry myself and put on my most impenetrable pyjamas, I rub my hand across the misty mirror and have a proper look. My hair is damp but not wet as I already washed it today. My eyes are bright. Of course they're bloody bright, I just had a massive orgasm, then thought I was going to be killed by a hoodie. That's two major adrenalin rushes within half an hour of each other. My skin looks better than it did a couple of months ago and I've definitely lost a bit of weight. I have a collarbone and less of a double chin. I don't think that's to do with diet so much as that I've started living again. I have a theory that people put on weight to protect themselves from pain. In my case from crushing boredom. After the reactions of Philo, Harry then Santo, I don't really think I need to obsess about weight so much, though. If I thought I needed to be skinny to attract a man then I was misguided.

I'm just about to get on my nightclothes when I spot something. It's a bite mark: a love bite at the base of my neck. Jesus, better cover that up. I have an old concealer in the bathroom cupboard and I spread some of it over the faint but defiant mark.

I visit Barney's room one last time to stroke his arm and kiss his cheek, before creeping into bed. The heating is off so Tommi had better get under the duvet in the next hour or he's going to die of exposure. I can't stop thinking of Santo's parting words as I got out of his car.

CHAPTER TWENTY SIX

'That wasn't so bad, was it?'

And it wasn't. But I made it too easy. He knew I was ripe for the plucking, the smooth bastard.

Where's Harry?

CHAPTER TWENTY SEVEN

Work this week has been bloody depressing. After a few months of good trade, there's now virtually nothing to do, too many people to do it and frankly, my heart isn't in it. So when lunchtime approaches and everyone is sloping off to sandwich shops and the like, I close the office door and have a few words with Elen.

She's wearing a charity-shop dress today, all green and yellow swirls, teamed with boots, a pink belt and bright pink lipstick. She looks fantastic. I'm wearing a mustard cowl-neck jumper to hide my 'bruise'. I managed to shrug it on with my new, well-fitting pinstripe trousers this morning before Tommi, the glue-eyed, moaning wreck in the bed next to me, could notice anything. I got dressed in the bathroom as it would have been awkward, anyway, getting ready in front of him. When I woke up, I had my back to him and he had his arm flung across my waist. I was careful not to scoot backwards in case I encountered a surprise morning glory, and as I ran to the bathroom to groom myself, I realised I'd awoken with a plan.

'Elen, how do you feel about taking over this pitch for me?'
Her eyes widen.

CHAPTER TWENTY SEVEN

'What, the boutique one?'

'Yup.'

I know it's a long shot. But she's always working for me instead of getting a proper chance herself. The boss would kill me if he knew I was handing something so high profile to a trainee. But I don't particularly care. It's not my fault Harry's not here. I miss Harry. I texted him again this morning but still no reply.

'Alice, are you allowed to let me do this?'

'I'm allowed to do anything I want. Mr Big left me in charge, remember?'

'Of course I remember. I'm surprised Belle hasn't actually stabbed you, she's so totally jealous.'

'Well, he was hardly going to give the phone-answering mentalist that responsibility, was he?'

'No, but positions of power are for men as far as she's concerned.'

'That's because she's a complete cocknocker. Look, here's what I've come up with so far. Something traditional with a touch of Victoriana. Not unlike your bedroom actually. Do what you like with it. I need to go out. I'll be back before we finish up today. Will you call me if anyone comes in with a query? Tell them I'm having a meeting across town.'

'Of course I will.'

She gets into my seat and I reach for my coat.

'Alice?'

'Yes?'

'What are you up to?'

I consider fobbing her off then decide against it.

'I'm going to meet up with Em.'

'*What*? Rabbit Face?'

'The very same.'

'Why?'

'She was on my road last night. I got back from a parents' drinks night and she was outside. Crying.'

'Oh my God. Do you think she might be dangerous?'

'I think she might be having a nervous breakdown. And I think Tommi's been lying.'

'But why do you have to see her?'

'I want to see her. She said something that stuck with me.'

'Like what?'

'Like I asked what she was doing and she said, "Ask him." And he was hiding in the spare room like some cowardy custard. There's a story there, obviously.'

(I still have her number after her charming texts, so I sent her a message this morning and she agreed to meet me. She suggested a pub. It's about twenty minutes away in a cab. I can't be arsed with the tube.)

'Okay. This is quite exciting, actually. You are such a dynamo.'

Elen dimples at me and studies the screen in front of her, already planning to take over the company, no doubt.

When I put my hand out for a cab, I fight off the tiniest doubt that this could be construed as going behind Tommi's back. The thing is, he's had his chance to come clean and now I'm going straight to the horse's mouth.

So to speak.

CHAPTER TWENTY-EIGHT

This place is one of those old men's pubs that young people think are vintage and cool. I quite like old men's pubs, but the wine is almost always horrible. In my experience, they have one choice each of red, white and pink. No fizz. And all of them are the flavour of vinegar. Apart from the pink. That usually tastes of candy floss and perfume.

Looking at the wine selection the prospects are grim, as expected, so I order a coffee. At least they've come on far enough to have a coffee filter on the go.

Rabbit Face – who is in jeans, converse and a parka – joins me at the bar and orders a pint of Guinness. I will never understand how anyone can drink that stuff. It tastes like tar. Em's hair is lank and her sockets are hollow.

'Hello Emma.'

She can't look me in the eye and stares at her hands.

'Hi.'

Her voice is barely there.

She seems so different to the vixen on the phone who was calling me a shit girlfriend. Maybe she really is having a nervous breakdown.

'Should we sit over there by the window?'

She gives a little nod.

As we make our way through the glare of low sunshine, I walk behind her, noting the way she slightly stoops. I wonder if that's because she's tall or because the troubles of the world are on her shoulders.

We sit opposite one another. She doesn't look at me and she doesn't say anything.

'Emma?'

She glances up. Her eyes fill with tears and she looks down again. Pulls a tissue out of her big pocket.

'God. I don't know why I came here.'

I try to sound reasonable.

'I was hoping you could tell me why you were outside our house last night. Why you were so upset?'

She takes a while to speak.

'Why do you think?'

She's not going to make this easy, obviously.

'Well. You were standing outside for ages in the freezing cold. You rang the bell enough to wake up my son, and messaged and called Tommi after he took the batteries out of the bell. That would suggest you're obsessed with him.'

Her head shoots up, pale eyes bloodshot.

'Obsessed. Is that what he says?'

'No. He says you're mad.'

She bursts into tears.

'The total bastard…'

She can't say anything else, she's so wracked with sobs. I scoot to her side of the table and put my arm around her. The bar girl looks over and I hold up my hand so she's knows it's okay. I can't imagine weeping young ladies are uncommon in bars.

CHAPTER TWENTY-EIGHT

At first Em is very stiff next to me, then she sort of caves in, like a badly baked cake.

'He's so cruel. And I love him so much.'

'How's he cruel, Emma?'

'He... he –'

She stops talking and cries more. I try to prompt her.

'I know you had a bit of naughtiness in the car.'

Oh God, I'm such a hypocrite.

'But that doesn't mean you're an item. I mean, you're so pretty you could have anybody. You don't have to set your sights on him.'

She is pretty. I only call her Rabbit Face because she has big, white teeth. Even her imperfections are pretty. She does have a honking voice though.

'Set my sights?' She wrings her tissue in her hands. 'He was so angry when I sent those texts to you, you know. I told him, I couldn't help it. I had to do something. I was losing him.'

'Huh?'

'He said if I caused any more trouble that would be it. Then he started ignoring my calls anyway. And I miss him *so* much.'

'A few drinks at lunchtime and a bit of flirtatious banter doesn't amount to a relationship, you know.'

She stares at me. She looks torn. I grow impatient.

'I don't know what you're hiding but you may as well spit it out.'

She squirms.

'I wanted to tell you. I would have told you last night if you'd been in... but by the time I saw you, I was so cold and felt so sad. I lost my nerve.'

'Tell me what?'

'He'll kill me. If I tell you then there really won't be any hope.'

'Christ, Emma, what is it?'

She takes a gulp of Guinness.

'That night... in the car. It's true, I didn't get drunk and he did. And I drove him home from the party. And I, you know...'

She stops again. Christ, it's like getting blood out of a stone.

'But it wasn't the first time. We've been seeing each other for over a year. He'd said he wanted to cool it for a bit. So I thought I'd remind him of how good we were together -'

'A year?'

She stops and takes another gulp of her Guinness.

'Wait there.' I jump up, slam a tenner down on the bar and point to some godforsaken Chardonnay. 'Biggest glass you have of that, please.'

When I return, she is still crying. Miserable tears rolling down her face. All at once, things are clearer. And it seems she's as much in the shit as me.

'I am so sorry, Emma.'

'What?'

'For all of this. I blamed you. But it takes two, doesn't it?'

She looks dumbfounded.

'You don't have to apologise to me.'

He was sleeping with her for a whole year. Why didn't I notice?

'Sorry to be nosy, but when the hell did you get the chance to spend time together? Apart from at work?

'His boys' nights at the pub every Thursday. That was really our night round my place. And sometimes at lunchtime, we'd come back early from the pub and do it in the stockroom.

The cheeky bastards.

'And you never got caught?'

CHAPTER TWENTY-EIGHT

'No. Nearly, once. But no. I think some people at work suspect. We were so close, until…'

She sniffles again. I can't believe what I'm hearing. I've never done it in a stock cupboard.

'Until?'

'A couple of months ago, I told him that I didn't want to creep around anymore. I wanted something more permanent. He didn't like that word. He still had sex with me at work sometimes, in the cupboard and sometimes in the loos when it was only me and him at the end of the day. But he stopped coming round on Thursdays. I put up with it for a few weeks, then it was the work party and I decided to try to win him back. Only it didn't work. He said I was trying to destroy his relationship with you. I mean, how could he blame me when he'd acted single for all of that time? Then, after he went to his mum's for the weekend, he came around one Sunday night. Said I had to leave him alone or he'd lose everything. That you'd thrown him out. Then he cried and we had sex and I thought there was hope.'

Tommi, you weak little idiot. No wonder she's all over the place.

Suddenly she's sobbing again. There really is no end to this girl's tears.

'He's smashed my head to pieces. I can't eat or sleep. It's a nightmare. And now I'm sitting here, pouring out my troubles to you. After everything I've put you through. I'm so so sorry.'

'It's okay.'

'It's not okay because I still love him and I still want him.'

'Really. It's okay. You've done me a favour.'

'How?'

I down more horrible wine. He had an affair for a whole

year. That is simply crazy. How could I not have noticed?

'I think he's more suited to someone your age than mine.'

'He doesn't think so.'

All at once she looks panicked.

'If you tell him about this conversation he will kill me. He told me that you and Barney are his life and that I'm just a stupid little girl. And I am. Because I believed him. I believed he loved me.'

Sobbing again. Jesus H Christ. I keep my voice even.

'Did he tell you he loved you?'

She closes her eyes then opens them again and has the good grace to look apologetic.

'Yes. Just before I asked for us to become a proper item. He said it while we…'

'Okay, okay.'

'Sorry.'

I pat her hand.

'It's not your fault.'

'Why are you being so nice to me? I haven't been nice to you.'

'I guess somebody has to be the grown-up. Annoyingly, that someone is me.'

I smile at her and she attempts to smile back, then looks at her watch.

'Oh, I have to get back to work. My lunch hour finished five minutes ago.'

'Well if I were you I'd wash my face in freezing cold water and get some concealer on. You currently look like you were caught in a house fire.'

She laughs at my sick joke. And just for a second I see the sunny, pretty girl that Tommi was having an affair with for

CHAPTER TWENTY-EIGHT

a whole twelve months. I get the feeling he thought he could get away with it, without her making any trouble. Obviously that's not how life works.

'You're actually really nice, Alice. And much prettier these days.'

She looks more closely at me.

'Younger looking.'

I don't say anything; my looks are no concern of hers. We may have just had a reasonable conversation but, still, she did have an affair with my partner.

As she stands she leans towards me.

'Please don't tell him I told you.'

'I won't.'

I go to the toilet which smells of mouldy towels and stale beer and lock the cubicle. Inside, I sit on the cracked toilet cover and bury my face in my shaking hands but I don't cry as much as I should because I'm not that surprised. Just disappointed. My mind keeps running the same question.

Why keep lying to me? Why lie?

After a while I open the door again and apply damage limitation to my crumpled face. Foundation and powder. My phone rings. After a bit I answer.

'Hey Elen. You okay?'

'Yes! I'm loving it, actually. I could get used to sitting in this chair!'

'I'll bet you could.'

She lowers her voice.

'Everything all right with Rabbit Face? You sound a bit weird.'

'She's gone.'

'And?'

I feel emptied out. I'm not ready to explain things.

'As suspected, she's mental and he's a wanker. Are you sure everything's okay there?'

'Totally. But, just so you know, Harry rang the office and asked if you were around. I told him you'd be back soon. He says he'll call again in half an hour. I can tell him you had to go home sick?'

My mind ticks.

'Could you please get a number I can reach him on, his usual one is dead. And give him my mobile number. Tell him I'll call him ASAP. There's somewhere I need to be first.'

'Alice?'

'It's okay. I'm not going to kill anyone.'

'Promise?'

'Scout's honour.'

CHAPTER TWENTY-NINE

I know I told Rabbit Face I'd keep schtum – sorry, Emma, I have to stop being such a bitch – but fuck that. I can't delay this. Tommi has lied and lied to me. It's time to draw a line under this complete shambles of a relationship.

When the cab stops outside his workplace, my stomach gives a lurch. I ignore it. I pay the driver, a nice man called Stan with white hair and a big, bobbly nose. I ring the doorbell to the main lobby with a beating heart and a jittery hand. Their receptionist is new so I have to explain who I am. When I enter she smiles. She looks about twelve and has a bonny face and giant hoop earrings. I tap my fingernails on my bag as she calls Tommi's extension. When he emerges through the office door with the frosted green window, he looks a little bewildered. I've only ever been to his office for 'functions' and a couple of times to drop off his keys when he forgot them, but I've never been there unannounced. He comes towards me and kisses my cheek. Well, kisses the air next to my cheek because I move slightly, realising that I don't want him to touch me.

'Can you spare five minutes, Tommi? For a coffee?'

There's a sandwich shop next door that does overly weak drinks with too much milk.

'Oh. Erm, okay. What's up?'

I flicker my eyes ever so slightly towards the receptionist who isn't even pretending not to listen. He realises.

'Lorraine, will you buzz the team and let them know I've had to pop out? They know what they're doing anyway. And they can get me on my mobile if they need me.'

She shoots him a soppy grin.

'Of course.'

Bloody hell. Another one mooning over him. I walk off ahead and he runs to catch up with me.

'Alice, what's up? What's happened?'

'Get us a seat.'

While he takes a small table in the window I order a couple of cappuccinos. He looks very edgy when I return.

'You're being really strange. What are you doing here? Is it about Emma last night? I'm so sorry about that. And I'm sorry I got so drunk. But she was really freaking me out and I was sad because I was home and you weren't there and I wanted to hang out and chat and –'

I hold up my hand.

'Tommi. The reason Emma was hanging about outside is that you were shagging her every Thursday night and in stock cupboards and God knows where else for ages. She thought you were a couple and she fell for you. Then you unceremoniously dumped her. How can you blame her? Most women don't fuck simply for fucking's sake. They fall in love.'

His eyes are saucers. Mine are stinging. For what we once were and the part I've played in what we are now. But also at the deceit. I blink hard in an attempt not to start weeping in front of two men in high-visibility jackets, studiously eating cheese and tuna jacket potatoes at the next table.

CHAPTER TWENTY-NINE

'Al, I've made so many mistakes but...'

'Don't, Tommi. If what is about to come out of your mouth is a lie, please don't. There's been enough dishonesty already.'

'It just happened. I was a fool. And when you start these things they're really difficult to get out of. She got so clingy. And she works with me. She could have got me sacked, then you would have found out. It became really difficult, trying to keep her sweet. I know it sounds weak but -'

'Tommi. I can't be with you anymore.'

'*What*? Alice, it's all been a stupid mistake. It's you I love: you and Barney...'

'Look, I know I lost it after he was born. I know I wasn't the fun girl you knew before. But that's the problem. We were in our twenties when we met. Now I'm more grown up. I don't want to be but I am. And you're not. We're simply not right for each other anymore. And bad feeling in the house is going to mess Barney up. Can't we try to be nice and work something out?'

He looks panicked.

'No we can't! We have to fight for this. We are right for each other. We just have to talk about it and start again.'

'And what if you're not the only one fancying other people?'

His brow furrows.

'What do you mean?'

'What I just said. What if I want to have fun? What if I want to catch up on all the years I stayed with one person, after a pitiful amount of lovers, while you sowed your wild oats on fake nights out with the lads?'

'What, so you're planning on becoming a good-time girl at thirty-nine? Since when did you become a slut?'

I slap him. The two guys in high-vis jackets turn into table-staring statues. Tommi grabs at his face like a true drama queen. I point at him across the table and he winces.

'Since I stopped feeling like a fucking packhorse. A fat donkey with a strict timetable and udders. What a nerve you've got, what a friggin' nerve. Not once have you come clean, apologised, begged to be forgiven for leaving me with the responsibility for everything while you waltzed off to the office and had a separate life with your new bit of stuff. You weren't having a fling, you were having a sodding relationship. She saw you more than I did. More than our son did. Well, fuck you.'

I jump up, sending my chair clattering to the floor, then grab my bag and storm off.

'Alice?'

He runs after me into the street.

'Don't. You had ample time to tell me the truth. Now there's nothing I want to hear from you.'

'But it's over. I ended it with her ages ago!'

I stop in my tracks.

'Really? So when I told you to keep it in your pants while I thought things through, you didn't go over there and fuck her again? You didn't mess her head up and reduce her to a Guinness-swilling wreck who still, after everything, wants to take you back?'

'Oh my God. Has she been talking to you? Have you met up?'

'It doesn't matter, Tommi. Just stop pissing around with her head. You have to apologise to her and realise you can't have another girl for all of that time and expect her feel nothing, or expect me to still want you!'

'Please. Please Alice. I have been the biggest twat on the

planet. And I've handled it terribly. But I honestly and truly didn't mean for it to happen like this. You and Barney are my world.'

I walk back to him and put my hand on the cheek I slapped.

'I don't hate you, Tommi. We used to be best mates. You still are my mate. And you're the father of my child. But we're just not right for each other anymore.'

When I see his face crumble, tears welling up in those lovely grey eyes, I turn and walk off down the road towards goodness knows where.

And it feels like I mean it.

CHAPTER THIRTY

As is happens, my walk isn't very long. I soon come across an alleyway I didn't know was there and turn down it, just to escape the general hubbub of the main street.

It's surprisingly pretty down here, like a side-road from another era. Cobbles and big old bricks. I like the sound of my boots on the cobbles and I like the sign hanging from the pub I've just come across, which looks like a place on a Christmas card. Little and oldie-worldy with a bay window.

The Bawdie House.

What a great name. Not that the name is terribly relevant right now. All I'm thinking of is the alcohol inside it; I just hope it isn't as grim as the stuff in the last bar. A nice cold fizz would be nice, but wine is wine and I need a little fortifier after that ridiculous display, just to clear the bullshit in my head.

I hit him. And, I mean, it's all very well telling your partner it's not working out. But what does this mean for Barney? We'll have to sell up, that's for sure, and I'll have to find me and my son a small flat or rent us a place until my half of the profit from our stupid, big house is all used up and we become bloody destitute.

CHAPTER THIRTY

With my head spinning, I climb the three whitewashed steps, through the faux antique door and into... bloody hell, into a totally fantastic little neon-filled cocktail bar with the best pink leather bar stools I've ever set eyes on and a happy-hour offer of two cocktails for six quid until seven p.m. It's only four o'clock so I'm well in.

Shit. I need to be on the tube by five.

The bar girl approaches. She's slim and tall with a platinum blonde quiff and no make-up. Only a twinkly-eyed elf like her could look so fab with hair that short. I feel, as I always have, a stab of envy for any woman who looks so naturally gorgeous and lithe. Then I remember that the slim thing has become less of an issue for me. What people find attractive isn't as limited as I used to think.

'Hey there. My first customer in an hour. What can I do for you?'

'Erm. I don't know. I like vodka. And citrus. What can you recommend?'

'Easy. Lemon Meringue Martini. My favourite.'

'Ooohh. That sounds nice.'

'Yup. Good looking and tasty.'

She winks. Why is she winking? I look down at my phone. No signal in here.

'Do you mind if I go outside and make a quick call while you make it?'

'No probs.'

I have to walk a little way down the alley to get a bar or two on my phone. When I finally call Marina, I establish she'd be perfectly happy to babysit for a few hours extra. I have no idea if Tommi will show up at the house after this latest revelation, but I don't want to see him and I don't want to risk not making it back by six.

'Thank you so much, Marina. If Tommi does come back earlier I'll still pay you as if you babysat until ten.'

She is well pleased. When I ring off I find missed calls on my phone. Six from Tommi. Two from an unknown number. Probably Tommi trying with someone else's phone. Three voicemails. I have no interest. I delete them. I'm glad I'm unreachable in The Bawdie House. I don't want to think about my real life right now. I want something good looking and tasty.

When I go back in, the martini is sitting on the bar. A lovely creamy yellow colour. I take a sip. The bar girl nods.

'Good, huh?'

'Delicious.'

'Well, be careful. It's easy to drink them fast.'

'I don't care. Make me ten more.'

'Oh dear. One of those days?'

I like her accent.

'Where are you from?'

'I'm Canadian.'

'Cool.'

'No. Not cool. London's way cooler. I'm Gracie.'

'Gracie. That's not a name you hear all of the time. I'm Alice. Your hair is fantastic.'

'Why thank you. Sorry you've had a bad day.'

'That's okay. I've come in here to make it better. Feed me drinks until I'm in a coma then put me in a taxi to hospital, please.'

'Dangerous.'

I look at her as she places a couple of glasses on the shelf behind her. She has a nice, genuine smile. If you're not going

CHAPTER THIRTY

to wear make-up it helps to have good teeth and good skin. She has both. As she reaches up, her top, a silky black and pink thing with a 'Bawdie House' badge, rides up, away from the top of black Capri pants and uncovers a stretch of pretty back. She turns and catches me admiring her. I quickly avert my gaze.

'You want another?'

I look at my glass. It's empty. I have no idea how.

'Yes, please. I'll savour the next one.'

She begins to mix.

When I was at uni I once had a crush on a girl. She was called Catrina and everyone had a crush on her. She was in third year when I was a fresher. She was clever and funny and gay and had bright turquoise hair and the most beautiful pale green eyes. One night at a party she told me I was gorgeous and kissed me on the lips, under an apple tree in the garden. It didn't last long because I was so buttoned up and freaked out, but I never forgot it and often regretted not kissing her properly. After she left she became a scientist and married a man. I was surprised to hear it. She was very successful with the ladies.

'Tell me why your day was shit.'

Her bluntness impresses me.

'I couldn't bore you like that, unless you were drinking too.'

She goes straight to the fridge, pulls out a beer, opens it and takes a swig.

'The boss is cool. Maximum two drinks on shift is what she says. This'll be my first.'

She clinks the bottle gently against my glass.

I like this bar.

So, as I sip my lemony drink, perched on my chrome and

pink leather stool, I give her a quick rundown of my meeting with Em, then my confrontation with Tommi. Often it's easier to open up to a stranger. A couple of older, masculine-looking ladies come in and order ciders as my tale unfolds, but apart from them we are pretty much uninterrupted. I even tell her about my crummy tally of lovers, my exhaustion at trying to keep the family running smoothly, and my unadventurous life to date.

She shakes her head.

'You're selling yourself short. You seem cool to me.'

'I am many things, Gracie. Cool isn't one of them.'

'Maybe you've become cool. How old are you?'

'I hate that question. I'm thirty-nine. Almost ready for the scrap-yard.'

She whistles.

'You love putting yourself down, don't you?'

'I'm a realist.'

'No, you're not. That's crap. Thinking like that will make you old. Thirty-nine isn't old and you don't look old. You're just bored. You need adventure.'

'Are you an adventurer?'

She flashes me another smile.

'I am. But I'm studying right now so I've slowed right down.'

'Really? What are you studying?'

'Teacher training, then a course on special needs.'

'Ooh. What got you into that?'

'My little brother has several issues and learning difficulties. He's amazing. I want to help other kids to realise their full potential. It can be hard on the families if they don't get help.'

'Bloody hell. What a brilliant thing to do with your life.'

'It's what I know. And anyway, I'm thirty-two now. I've

CHAPTER THIRTY

done the travelling thing. I've done the falling in love inappropriately and wasting time thing. Now I'm doing the stuff for my future. And for my brother.'

'I wish I'd been as wise as you at your age. I'm a fucking loser.'

She begins to shake another drink.

'Quit feeling sorry for yourself. You probably did what you thought was wise at the time. Life always fucks you, one way or another...'

She puts another martini in front of me.

'This one's on me. A commiseration. Though it does sound like you can still have that man of yours back if you want him. If you *reaally* want him.'

She smiles again. Holds my eye. She's very striking with her rosy lips, platinum hair and light brown eyes. I've not met many people with light brown eyes.

I need to make this my last drink.

'Thank you very much.'

Her fingers lightly brush mine as she pushes it towards me and I take it.

'I wish I could have a job I loved.'

'You don't like your job?'

'I don't care about it. I'm in a corporate office dealing with vain clients who talk shit. I want to work for myself.'

'Do it then.'

'It's not that easy.'

'Yes it is. Being miserable is actually easiest. But then, saying "fuck it, why not?" is quite easy too.'

We chat for quite a while. A few more women wander in. No men so far. It's pushing six o'clock. I should go home and see my son. Suddenly a very thin woman also in a black and pink top, but with black cargo pants, a pony tail and lots of facial piercings appears at the bar. Black and pink is obviously the uniform of this place. She smiles at Gracie who smiles back.

'Hey there! Quiet one?'

Gracie nods.

'Been chatting with my friend here or I'd have gone into a coma. Alice, this is Frances. Frances runs this place. She's an actual slave driver.'

Francis gets behind the bar and pretends to clip her around the ear.

'Don't listen to her, Alice. Doesn't do a scrap of work this one.'

I like their easy camaraderie.

'You sure you don't mind doing tonight?'

Gracie shrugs.

'Course I don't. Extra money never goes amiss.'

'See you later.'

Gracie comes from behind the bar.

'I've got two hours then back on shift.'

'Oh wow. Well, thank you for the chat and for introducing me to my favourite cocktail.'

'You're welcome.'

She regards me.

'Come upstairs and I'll give you something to eat so you don't hurl on the way home.'

She takes my hand and I grab up my bag as she leads me out of the pub and to a front door right next to it.

'You know, I should be getting along. I'll probably just hail a cab -'

'Nonsense, come and see the flat. It's great.'

CHAPTER THIRTY

And with that, I'm through the door, up the narrow stairs and through another door into a small, perfect apartment. I say apartment because it has high ceilings and a little balcony overlooking the alleyway and is simply too cool to be referred to as a 'flat'. Maybe I just think everywhere that isn't my big, boring house is fabulous. But this place definitely rocks. It is painted bright white, to maximise the light, I'm guessing, and she has purple furniture. A giant purple sofa, purple easy chair, violet drapes by the bright balcony windows. The prints on the walls are all boldly coloured abstracts.

'Oh *God*, I love this.'

The light outside is almost gone so she switches on a lamp in the corner.

'It's Frances who decorated it. She owns it. She lives in the other one upstairs. She let me rent this because she knows I won't trash it.'

'It's adorable.'

She goes to a small bright red fridge (which is in the living room, how cool) and takes out a couple of cheeses, adds a loaf of uncut bread, butter and knives then puts it down on the coffee table.

'Help yourself.'

'I don't know if I'm hungry.'

'No?'

She produces a bottle of vodka and a carton of juice from the fridge.

'At least get some vitamins from the juice. It's tropical!'

She mixes us both a vodka and juice.

'Gracie, can I ask a question?'

'Of course.'

She hands me my drink.

I perch on the purple sofa. She does too, kicking off her pumps and curling her long legs under herself.

'Is the pub downstairs a… erm… gay bar?'

She laughs.

'What do you think?'

'Well, the clientele were all women and …'

'Of course it is! You've never been before?'

'No, I chanced upon it. I've not been frequenting new bars very much over the past few years. Well, I hadn't been until recently. Now I seem to be catching up, somewhat.'

'What a shame. I hoped you'd come in looking for some company.'

Now I know for sure. She's flirting and she sort of has been since I walked into the bar. I may be slightly woozy, but not pissed enough not to know what I'm doing. What the hell am I playing at coming up here?

'Ha. Do I even look gay?'

'I don't know if there is a 'look', Alice. You do get very glamorous lesbians, you know.'

'Are you calling me glamorous?'

'Hell yeah! You're hot.'

'Am I?'

Will I ever stop being flattered by being called 'hot'?

'Don't be ridiculous, of course you are. You're dark and mysterious. My total opposite.'

'I'm your total opposite because you're taller, slimmer, more toned, have broader, more exciting horizons and are infinitely better looking.'

'You think so?'

She scoots closer to me. I try to back away without seeming rude, but the arm of the sofa stops me.

CHAPTER THIRTY

'Well, you certainly give a lot of compliments for a straight girl.'

'It's just the truth.'

She leans forward and kisses me on the cheek.

'Thank you.'

'What for?'

'Making my day.'

I become slightly breathless.

'I'm starting to feel weird.'

'Good weird or bad weird?'

'Scared weird.'

'I have that effect.'

I laugh nervously then catch a whiff of her cologne. Something woody. Her eyes are on me so I look at her collarbone. She has a long neck. Unblemished skin. *Must stop looking at her neck.* I look at my knees.

'So, Alice. I have had a really nice time talking to you and I didn't want to let you leave. What does that mean?'

'I'm not gay, you know.'

She laughs. It's loud and quite infectious.

'I don't fancy lesbians all that much.'

'Eh? Then how do you ever have sex?'

'Not all straight women are as straight as they say they are.'

She scoots even closer. I try to protest.

'I've been copping off with more than my fair share of blokes recently.'

'So?'

'So I'm a heterosexual slag.'

'Maybe you're just finding your feet. Maybe you don't know what you are.'

'I've never even kissed a woman. Well, not properly.'

'Seriously?'

She is so cheeky. I like her.

'Well, Alice, seeing as you're going through a few changes, why not add another experience to the list?'

'Like what?'

'Like let me kiss you. Just once.'

'I'm scared.'

'You don't need to be. How about you relax, see if you like it and leave if you don't?'

I can't argue with this. Don't want to if I'm honest.

'Oh fuck it.'

She laughs again. Then she leans forwards and kisses me.

She tastes of Tesco tropical juice and her lips are soft as marshmallows. It's strange not feeling any stubble as we kiss, and also, admittedly, rather erotic. Soon the soft slow kiss becomes something else and her tongue is in my mouth. Any thought of legging it disappears as her perfume envelops me and her tongue dances. She's so gentle but totally in control. I like it. We kiss for a long time. I hardly dare move at first, then I place one hand on that long slender neck and another at the base of her spine. She feels like satin.

Her top has slightly risen as she leans forward and without even thinking, my hand creeps up her back. It is silky and warm.

'Gracie. I've never done anything like this before...'

Her voice has lowered somewhat as she kisses my face, 'You're doing fine.'

Her hands move to either side of my neck.

'Are you okay?'

I am very okay. I don't reply, just pull her to me, kissing her harder than before. It doesn't feel weird, it feels good.

CHAPTER THIRTY

Suddenly she grabs my thighs and guides me into straddling her. She's stronger than I expected. Still kissing her, and feeling her hands stroking over my pinstriped buttocks, I reach behind to my feet and push off first one boot then the other. She takes my hand and places it over her heart. I know what she wants and after a moment's hesitation I find I can't help myself. Tentatively, I stroke over her clothes, until one fingertip then another, touches her breast and her hardening nipple.

She inhales sharply, as I do, and whispers into my hair, 'That's so good.'

Hearing it emboldens me. Shocking even myself, I kiss down her neck, breathing her in, and nuzzle the exposed skin at the front of her shirt. Her smell is feminine and intoxicating. I notice that her buttons are actually press studs. Christ, I can't resist. I really can't. I undo the first, kiss her mouth, then undo the second. After the third I can see for sure that she's wearing no bra. It gives me a thrill that I hardly understand. I undo the other two press studs, and then, like opening a present, I push the fabric aside to reveal her small, beautiful breasts. I can hardly believe how perfect they are. How different from my own.

Awed, I cover them both with my hands, feeling the stiff buds against my palms, and touch them like I enjoy my own to be touched, before taking one of them gently into my mouth. When I suck, Gracie lets out a groan that is so sweet I feel my heart begin to play a samba. I suck the other, loving her reaction, loving the power I have. Without even thinking about it, as I lick and caress, I reach one hand between her legs and rub against the fabric of her trousers. So strange, no bulge, just heat.

She gasps, and in a sudden move she grabs the bottom of my jumper and, pushing me upright, rips it over my head. She smiles when she sees my own ample breasts straining against the lace of my old bra. As I caress her, she reaches expertly behind me and snaps it open. Soon, as she begins to explore them with her mouth, my groans begin to match hers.

'Christ, Alice, you are so beautiful.'

She wraps her arms around me so we are skin to skin and kisses me deeply once more. Then she whispers, 'I want to take your trousers off, but you bi-curious ladies usually get scared right about now. You like boobs but the rest of it terrifies the shit of you.'

I like the way she says 'boobs'.

'I don't know anything about bi-curious. I only came out for a drink.'

She laughs. I want to take off the rest of her clothes. What the fuck is happening to me? All at once I'm unbuttoning and unzipping her. She is wearing little, black, cotton shorts. My mind is exploding. I slip my hands into the back of her knickers. I have my hands on a girl's backside. It's smooth and curved and warm. She pushes her pants off, revealing a blond triangle of hair at the top of long, lithe legs, and then unzips my jeans so that in no time at all we're naked.

This is the first time I falter. I'm scared about what to do next. She, of course, isn't. Aroused and unhesitating, she climbs on top of me, pressing the length of her body against mine. For a moment she caresses my breasts again as we kiss, then lightly moves her hand downwards and slips a finger inside me. It's such a shock, the jolt of electricity that shoots through me, that I flinch.

'Are you okay?'

CHAPTER THIRTY

I can hardly breathe.

'I'm fucking amazing.'

I move my own hand, and as she begins to massage me with her fingers, I place it between her legs and insert it into her soft wetness. She feels so hot and alive. When she throws her head back I kiss her neck as we both move to each other's rhythm. What shocks me is how much I'm ready to climax. I cannot get enough of her. She knows exactly what to do and suddenly, almightily, I start to judder. Within seconds I am jerking against her and making sounds I didn't even know I was capable of. After I've climaxed it takes a little while to get my breath back. She smiles and kisses me.

'How was that?'

I don't know what to say. It was simply incredible. And a total surprise. I kiss her gently, then more firmly and move back to her nipples, taking them between my teeth, cupping her bottom as I do so.

'We're not finished.'

I don't have the confidence to do what I'd like to do to her, I'm too scared I might be rubbish at cunnilingus, so I kiss the blonde downy hair, then reinsert my fingers and gently search for what I know is there. With a little careful listening, I work out where she likes to be touched best, probably that pesky love button that I didn't even know about before, and I move my hand, slowly at first then more and more quickly. Her gasps are amazing.

I am making her make those sounds.

I am more shocked at myself right at this moment than I have ever been in my life. And I feel myself become re-aroused as her cries build to a crescendo and her whole body flexes and gyrates then relaxes backwards into the sofa.

When she eventually speaks she sounds stunned.

'Have you done this before?'

I lay my body against hers again and kiss her shoulder, marvelling at her gorgeous little breasts, wishing mine were so neat, wishing I had time to arouse those nipples again with my tongue.

'Of course I haven't. I'm straight. And un-sexual. I don't even do it to myself.'

She laughs.

'But I am slightly pissed.'

'I noticed.'

'And I'm totally freaked out that I just got naughty with a girl. A sexy, gorgeous, female girl.'

She wraps her arms around me and looks in my face.

'We kissed your make-up off. You look fucking phenomenal.'

'Thank you.'

'Welcome. I've got to go and do my shift soon. You want to stay? I have the most beautiful dildo in the world, called Charlotte, and some nice silk ties. Boy, we could have some fun.'

I have never used a dildo. She's got a name for hers. And incredibly, the thought of it turns me on. But I can't.

'Shit, Gracie, I've got a sitter at home waiting for my return. And a son who has not been getting enough of my attention lately. I'm so sorry.'

She kisses the palm of my hand.

'Don't be sorry, I'm the one who's sorry that I won't be able to get my hands on all of this again, later.'

She strokes a leisurely middle finger down my body. I sigh. Then I reluctantly get up and begin to gather up my clothes.

'You must think I'm such a slut.'

CHAPTER THIRTY

'I love sluts.'

'This slut has a whole other life. And I need to get back asap.'

'Don't worry, I'll order you a cab. They're cheap and they're quick.'

CHAPTER THIRTY-ONE

The cab isn't the only thing that's cheap and quick.

The afterglow of what just happened begins to turn into something else precisely ten minutes into the cab journey. Gracie gave me her card and a plastic 'hot cup' with a black coffee in it, so I'd reach home in some state of composure. As I sip, it sinks in that I just had a one-night stand (well, one-evening stand) with a girl after having a one-night stand with Santo last night. I think of a song by a crazy female singer that Tommi has on his iPod. I always thought he liked these musicians just to seem hip, but actually she sings a naughty song about fucking pain away that suddenly seems very fitting.

Is that what I'm doing? Four sexual 'partners' in such a short time. None of them my actual partner. And since when did I fancy women? I don't think I do. I just fancy Gracie. I mean, for Christ's sake, she mentioned her dildo and had me licking my lips. This is horrendous. I'm definitely having a nervous breakdown. I've split up with Tommi and shagged a woman on the same day, and all before eight p.m.

I just need to get into my fleecy pyjamas, make some hot chocolate and, for a treat, let Barney stay up late with me and watch whatever film he wants.

CHAPTER THIRTY-ONE

In fact, that's a plan, right there.

CHAPTER THIRTY-TWO

Plan schman.

The minute I walk in, I hear music from the kitchen and smell something cooking. As I enter, Tommi is finishing a glass of wine and stirring a pan, Barney is eating ice cream and there's a giant bunch of lilies in my favourite vase on the table.

What the hell is he up to? His eyes are slightly bloodshot but he pushes a smile onto his face.

'Well hello!'

Barney swivels on his chair and beams.

'Mummy! Daddy bought you flowers! Aren't they pretty?'

He jumps down and runs at me, gives me a mega-squeeze, then runs back to his ice cream.

'Very nice. When did you get here?'

'About seven. I went shopping first. Making your favourite.'

'Green curry, Mummy!'

'Barney Boo, after your ice cream, would you like to watch a film upstairs with some bed snacks?'

'No! Daddy said I could stay up!'

'Did he?'

'Sorry Al, I wasn't quite sure what time you'd be back.

CHAPTER THIRTY-TWO

Working late?'

There's a slightly manic glint in Tommi's eye. I don't know why he's behaving like nothing's happened, but using Barney as a shield by letting him stay up is pretty low.

'Actually no. I went for a drink all on my own. Just wanted to have a little think.'

The glint intensifies.

'I called you.'

'Sorry. No signal in there.'

'Well listen, kick off your shoes, sit down and let us pamper you. Right Barney?'

'*Righto* Daddy!'

'While I serve up, why don't you have a little drinkie?'

He takes ice from the freezer and fills my transparent ice-bucket. Then he opens the fridge and produces a fifty quid bottle of fizz. This is getting stranger by the minute. He pops the cork, fills a flute with sparkling liquid and brings it to me. He then fills another flute with orange juice and hands it to a delighted Barney.

He puts plates down on the table and places the pot of curry and bowl of rice on coasters in the centre. I think the last time he made food for me was two years ago. It was a cheese toastie. He fills his own flute and salutes me, before taking a sip.

'Why don't you sit down?'

My stomach is in knots. This is so surreal. Did I imagine what I said to him today or has he finally gone over the edge?

I sit. Barney also sits and Tommi joins us. Barney keeps smiling excitedly at me then Tommi.

'Daddy says he has a surprise!'

'Shh Barney. A surprise means you don't say anything.'

'What's going on, Tommi?'

'I... I just wanted to say, to you and to Barney, that I'm sorry. Sorry for not being around enough, sorry for always being out or at work, sorry Mummy has worked so hard at home without enough thanks, sorry I haven't walked you to school enough Barney.'

'That's okay Daddy. Isn't it, Mummy? Men work very hard, don't they?'

Oh yes. So hard.

'We all work quite hard, Barney-Boo.'

I can't believe he's laying all of this on me with our son in the room. I want to strangle him.

'So, erm, anyway. I really really want to be a better dad and a better... man... for you, Alice. And I want to make my family proud. So today I spoke to Rob at work, and he's agreed that when the new premises open next month I'll work there, helping train up the team he's putting together and Spike will take over my job.'

He looks meaningfully at me.

'So I'll be working with a whole new bunch of people. And I told him I'd have to leave by five at least twice a week and he said that was fine.'

'That's nice.'

Barney doesn't really get why this is news and has started steering a red Hot Wheels car around the plates.

'Also, Alice. I have taken you for granted. If you can find it in your heart to forgive me, Barney and I would like to know -'

He awkwardly fumbles in his pocket. Barney looks up, 'What would we like to know?'

'Tommi?'

My throat is sealing up. Please no. He wouldn't, surely? A

CHAPTER THIRTY-TWO

small box is produced. He opens it. A pretty, tasteful diamond on a simple band.

'Will you marry us?'

Barney begins to laugh. A big, throaty chuckle that goes on for at least a minute.

'Daddy, I can't marry Mummy. She's my mummy.'

He keeps on laughing.

'Alice?'

He has the fevered look of a lunatic. Or that's how it seems to me. What the *fuck* was he thinking? Did he buy that thing on the way home?

I fix Tommi with a razor-sharp glare that turns him slightly pale, then paste on a smile and rub Barney's head.

'You're right, Barney. That would be silly, wouldn't it? Mummies can't marry crazy, giggling loons called Barney, can they?'

'Noooo!'

'Listen, Barney, Daddy and I want to talk about some boring getting-married stuff, so would you like to take some Jelly Babies upstairs and watch *Monster House* in bed for a bit?'

'Sweeties at bedtime?'

'Just this once.'

'WOW. Yes please.'

I grab the sweets from Barney's special jar and he takes them. I never give him sweets before bed and he's already had ice cream so he's super-amazed. I lead him up the stairs like a docile little lamb, as he carefully keeps his treasure safe in his cupped hands. Soon he's cross-legged and chewing and the film is about to begin.

'Thank you so much, Mummy. Did you know, Oliver at school says getting married is for losers?'

'I think it is, too.'

'Daddy doesn't.'

'He used to. I'm sure he'll change his mind.'

'You're too young to get married, Mummy.'

'Too right!'

He sniggers and I kiss him on the head.

'I'll be checking on you in half an hour. Have to clean the sugar off those teeth.'

'Okay. Love you.'

'Love you too.'

CHAPTER THIRTY THREE

'What are you doing?'

I have closed the kitchen door behind me and I'm hissing like an alley cat.

'Didn't we break up today?'

He is sitting, slumped at the table. I don't feel sorry for him because that's what he wants me to do.

'Why did you bring Barney into it like that? Are you crazy?'

'I didn't know what else to do. I just wanted to show you how much I love you. Both of you.'

'You just wanted to keep Barney in the room because you're a damn coward. Barney already knows you love him. And what kind of doormat would I be if I saw a bit of bling and immediately forgot what's been going on in your "other" life?'

'I don't know you anymore. You're so harsh.'

'Oh, get lost. All that's happened is my eyes have opened. I used to let you off with everything. Now I don't. Imagine how much we might have put things right if you'd thrown all of the energy you used in covering up your affair into making us into a closer family. You are a guttersnipe, Tommi. A weak, cowardly, lazy bastard.'

'I've changed. I've already got a job somewhere else. I won't be in an office with Em, just like you said I shouldn't. We could take a holiday together. We could find our old selves. Barney's old enough to stay with his grandparents for a few days on his own. Let's just do it. It could be the making of us.'

'If you'd said that six months ago, I would have been very happy. If you'd simply come home a night or two by six it would have been a start. But you didn't. You've been living like a single man while I did all the boring, difficult stuff and now you're panicking about losing your comfortable life. It's bullshit. I don't trust you anymore.'

'You don't trust me? You're the one who's decided to become a prostitute.'

Oh my God. He's a prize, this one.

'Why the hell would you want to marry a prostitute?'

'Do you want this curry or not?'

'Why are you bringing curry into it?'

'I just slaved over that.'

'Bully for you. You cooked one meal in how many years?'

Tommi starts to cry. Why is he always weeping these days? I'm all for men having a feminine side but his only seems to have conveniently developed in the last fortnight.

'I know I've been rubbish at all of that but you've been a moody, narky cow for the past few years. How come you've just started being your old self now?'

I sit down. He has a point. But talking about it would just be opening another can of extremely volatile worms.

'We had a child, Tommi.'

He reaches his hand across the table and puts it on my mine. I take a swig of this rather tasty champagne.

'We were great as carefree lovers. I was younger and energetic and loved funfairs and going to the cinema. But

CHAPTER THIRTY THREE

then this gorgeous, cheeky, knackering child came along; and by the time he was two I couldn't just head off to the pub with you and have a giant glass of wine. Because you would have a pint and read the paper and I would be running after Barney. That's how it's been ever since.'

'Oh come on. I've done my bit -'

'You've done *a* bit. The first time you took Barney somewhere for more than an hour without me was to your mum's a few weeks ago. And that nearly finished you off.'

'You're better at it than me.'

'No, I'm not. I just haven't had the choice of being the lazy one. And now I'm doing better because I've suddenly had help.'

'Can't we work at things? We've been together fourteen years.'

'Too long. I don't think people should settle down in their twenties. Not if they haven't lived enough.'

'Please don't say that.'

'I want us to live apart.'

'*No.*'

His blubbing intensifies.

'*Pleease.*'

Now I'm thinking maybe this crying is real. Maybe he does feel sorry and want us to stay together.

'Tommi. Funding this fucking house and your stupidly expensive Little Shit car and Barney's childcare and after-school clubs and everything else is *killing* us. I don't want worry any more, I don't want stress. I don't want to feel old.'

'Do you even like the ring?'

I look at it, sitting there, all forlorn, just like its purchaser. And it is a pretty thing; but I feel nothing. I should feel sad or angry or sorry or something. I just feel it was a stupid idea and a good indication of why we aren't right for each other.

'It's a lovely ring. It's just too late.'

He stands.

'You've broken my heart.'

I stare at him in disbelief.

'And you didn't break mine?'

'No. I can tell. You're not upset enough. I think you're having an affair.'

'Don't be bloody ridiculous.'

He picks up his jacket.

'I'm going out.'

The door closes decisively behind him.

I sit on my own and stare into space. What a mess.

After five minutes I finish my glass and pop upstairs. Barney is awake. I've stuffed my pockets with Jelly Babies. I squeeze into his bed and watch the film with him as we munch on sweeties. I refuse to think about anything. The logistics of selling up and moving on are just too mind-blowing. Instead I fall asleep bathed in blue TV light, with Barney snuggled into me, and only wake up in the early hours when his constant fidgeting nudges me out of the bed and onto the floor.

Then I crawl back to my own room and sleep, spread out like a giant starfish, fully clothed and with fuzzy teeth.

And Tommi doesn't come back.

CHAPTER THIRTY-FOUR

Tommi's parents are lovely. Eva and Gus. I have always thought they were nice, if a little too indulgent. Both of their sons, to my mind, had too much done for them. Spoiled. But only because Eva will do anything for anyone. That's why I'm surprised there's a hardness to Eva's voice when I answer the phone. When I look at the clock, it's 7.50 a.m.

'Alice?'

'Eva.'

'Did I wake you?'

'No, I was just making Barney's breakfast for school.'

I'm lying. I was asleep. Barney was also flat-out from being up so late. Though I'm sure the phone will have woken him.

'Are you all right, Eva? You sound upset.'

'I'm calling about Tommi. Well, you and Tommi. He phoned me at two o'clock this morning. He sounded drunk. He said you'd split up. He said he was thrown out of his own house and that you were...'

'I was what?'

'That you - have you found someone else?'

Argh. That lying little mummy's boy.

'He said he asked you to marry him last night, but that you

wanted to be with other people.'

'WHAT?'

Now, I know in films this is the bit where I'd be so shocked I wouldn't explain properly and I'd put the phone down and there'd be a whole half hour where Tommi's parents believed me to be the bad guy and then it would all come out at the end. But this is no cheesy rom-com and I am no doormat. Not anymore.

'Eva. I'm sorry to be the one to tell you this, you know I love you. But you have to steel yourself for what you're about to hear. Tommi has been having an affair for over a year. It's a girl from his work. I found out just before your birthday weekend. Through her. He said it was a one-off night but it turns out it wasn't at all.'

She gasps.

'That's why I haven't been to see you. I was too upset and I didn't want to spoil your celebration. Also, just so you know, I asked him to give me some space to get over the shock and he immediately went to her flat and had sex with her again. I know this happened because she told me, and he admitted it. Sort of.'

I know that's low but I have to let her know how serious this is.

'Alice. I had no idea…'

She sounds like she's about to cry.

'Look, I've been struggling with working and not seeing Barney, for a long time. I've also struggled with the lack of help from Tommi. Having no bloody life has made me moody and angry. I can see why he wanted someone easier to handle than me.'

'I can't believe he had an affair.'

CHAPTER THIRTY-FOUR

'This is the second time, Eva. He was messing with Tess before I had Barney.'

'*No!*'

'I know.'

There's a silence.

'You're sure?'

'Positive.'

'Oh, Alice. Can you forgive him?'

'The sex, yes. The lies, no. I think he's a big, lying baby.'

She sounds very forlorn.

'He's always been young in his mind. I thought that was one of the reasons you loved him.'

'It was. But not now. He asked me to marry him to keep me, that's all. It was a desperate act, Eva. I don't think he really knows what he wants.'

'But Barney...'

'I know. I'm sorry. There's nothing I can say... but... but... I'm sure we can make this as easy as possible on him. Barney loves you guys so much. So do I. You'll see him as much as always, I mean I'll bring him myself when Tommi's busy. You're my family, too. And I'll change my work hours and pick him up from school more. And Tommi will have to spend more proper time with him, if he has him for weekends.'

Suddenly it hits me, the enormity of what I'm saying, and I start to cry. I didn't come from a broken home. Whatever the circumstances, I have now failed. And Barney is going to be the victim of that failure. I can hardly believe it. What if we move and he *hates* it?

'Alice, don't cry. I'm so sorry you've been going through this. As long as we all try to be kind to each other, Barney will be fine. He has us and his cousins and your parents and you know Tommi loves him, don't you? And you. You know that.'

'Yes. I do know. I'm just so shocked that he could lie so well. He's usually so bad at it. Or I thought he was.'

Now Eva is sobbing.

'What a shame, Alice. What a stupid shame. Do you think things could be repaired? Do you think?'

'No.'

'Do you want us to come over? To help?'

'Thank you, no. I'll get him to school then my mum is coming tonight. She doesn't know yet. She thinks she's babysitting so Tommi and I can have a night out. I have no idea how to tell her.'

'You'll find the right words.'

'Thank you for not being nasty to me.'

She lowers her voice.

'Gus wasn't my first love, you know. He was the one after the man who broke my heart. Much as I love my son, an affair is hard to forgive. But don't totally close off from it. This might be the moment he starts growing up.'

'I'd better get Barney into his uniform. I'll call you over the weekend, Eva.'

'Okay, love. I'm very very sorry this has happened. And I know Gus will be too. Big kiss to Barney.'

'Will do.'

I don't want to help Tommi grow up. I already have a child, I don't want two. I text Smithy. He's the only one who gets it.

It's over Smithy. He was fucking her for a year. That's enough.

I don't expect him to be awake. But my inbox pings a moment later.

That's my girl. He was never good enough for you. If

CHAPTER THIRTY-FOUR

you get back together, I never said that.

I laugh. How can I be laughing now?

CHAPTER THIRTY-FIVE

I bloody knew this was on the cards. I arrive at work and there's nothing to work on.

'All contracts frozen'.

There is in an email from big Mr Benham. He's coming in at 10:30 a.m. for a meeting. Everyone is twiddling their thumbs and we all know something big is happening. I am sitting in Harry's office and Elen is in the loos tidying up her make-up, because she got upset when she heard about the meeting. After all it can only be one thing. Oh fuck. Much as I don't like it, I need this job.

When Mr Benham comes in, all pastel *Charlie's Angels* suit and Joop, I smile and stand. I'm wearing a wrap dress with boots and his eyes flick up and down, then he nods.

'Good colour on you. Very Spanish.'

'Thank you. Would you like a coffee?'

'No thank you, Alice. I think I should cut to the chase. I'm afraid the company is in trouble. Before it gets any worse I've decided to cut my losses. Sorry.'

'Oh. Very to the point.'

He laughs.

'You're a funny girl. I'm so sorry I can't offer you a job

CHAPTER THIRTY-FIVE

somewhere else, but I'm sticking with my American interests now. Unless you want to move to the US of A?'

'No thanks. That's okay.'

It's not really okay but it seems the right thing to say.

'I'm afraid this is my last business in London and it just isn't pulling its weight. We lost the Hoxton contract last week. Nobody's fault. They just decided they didn't want to spend the money right now. And if a place is limping I have to let it go.'

'I don't blame you.'

'No?'

'No. Life's too short.'

'Well that's mighty magnanimous of you.'

He glances at the door, as if to check that bat-ears aren't listening, then leans towards me.

'And because I'm cutting my losses as of right now, the least, and if I'm honest, the most, I can do is half a year's wage to each employee. I know it isn't much but it's more than a lot get when a place folds.'

'We're closing today?'

'Uhuh.'

I gulp.

'I see. Well, it gives us all six months to look elsewhere, Mr Benham. It's better than nothing. Though I think one or two of the others might have something to say...'

I glance through the slats at Belle, who is glaring at my closed door. Who the fuck will she annoy now?

I am experiencing a surprising reaction to the news. Along with the worry, there's also a rather surprising little nugget of relief and maybe even excitement nestling in the pit of my stomach. I don't have to stay here and I don't have to resign.

I'm being pushed. Forced into a new start. Bloody hell. It's all going on. Surely all of this weirdness and change is going to turn into a big pile of jibbering fear, soon?

'Alice?'

My head is whirring. It keeps doing that.

'Yes. Sorry.'

'Let's tell them. I don't like drawing out unpleasantness. Any complaints or questions, my solicitors can handle. I have to leave the country at noon.'

Wow. He's cold. Suddenly I see where Melissa gets it from. I like his directness though. And he's right. You hear about people turning up for work to find the doors locked and wages stopped forthwith. It could definitely be worse.

'Mr Benham?'

'Yes?'

'What happened to Harry?'

My Benham's tanned face suddenly blanches.

'Harry decided he needed a new direction in life.'

'Oh. Is he okay?'

'I don't know. And to be honest, I don't think I'm the one to ask.'

Blimey. I know the 'mucky touching' in his office was inappropriate but he's my friend and I hope he's all right.

CHAPTER THIRTY-SIX

I can't believe I'm in a pub again. And I can't believe we gave everyone else the slip. They were all devastated and Belle wouldn't shut up, so we ran for it. Elen is inconsolable. This last week she got a taste for the job. My job to be precise. I think she'd started imagining being the head designer at Benham's.

We jumped in a cab to Camden and we are in a gastro pub because The Dog isn't open yet. So much has happened since our evening there. But it feels very different by day. And it's only eleven a.m. For a change I'm being sensible and drinking coffee, but Elen isn't and has downed most of a very large glass of red. Her mascara is smudged.

'I've loved working with you, Buggy. And so many of my friends are struggling to find a good job. What am I going to do?'

'Go on holiday. You can afford your rent for a while, so just go and clear your head. That's what I would do. Go for a month then spend five months finding your next job.'

'What if I can't?'

'You're not even twenty-five yet. It doesn't matter if you can't! You're pretty and healthy, that's all you need right now.

Everything is a potential adventure. I wish someone had told me that at your age. Not that I'd have listened.'

'What about you? What will you do?'

I shrug.

'Six months wages will be a nice little buffer, but I don't have a clue. I don't even know where I'll be living. Not with Tommi and not at that house. That's all I know.'

'Oh my *God*. So it's properly over then?'

'Of course it is…'

'I'm sorry.'

'Don't be. It's been a long time coming.'

As I speak she looks out of the window over my shoulder and her eyes widen. She gives a little, begrudging wave. A bunch of achingly hip young people, headed by a girl of about nineteen with flowing red hair, minuscule denim shorts, fishnet tights and bright red lipstick are coming down the street in a troupe. Behind them come a couple of handsome boys in ripped jumpers and jeans and last, but by no means least, comes Philo in a flowing white shirt and dress pants. They should all be freezing cold but don't seem to be showing any sign of it.

'Hi Elen!'

The girl has a strong London accent.

'Hi Erica. How are you?'

The girl's eyes sweep over me then dismiss me like I'm a shadow.

'I'm good. What's up? Hoped to see you last night.'

Elen whips up the best smile she can.

'Oh sorry. It was a school night. Early for work and all that. What you up to?'

I look at Philo who smiles at me. He looks thinner than last time and a little tired. Still amazingly pretty, though.

CHAPTER THIRTY-SIX

'All kipped at Philo's after the gig, didn't we, darlin'?'

She blows a kiss at Philo who smiles and nods. Then he glances at me and winks. Naughty boy. Erica doesn't see the wink, but she picks up on something.

'So Elen, is this your mum?'

Elen stares at her.

'Of course, she's not my mum.'

'Oh, sorry.'

'Fucking hell, Erica, my mum's fifty. Are you mental?'

Erica smirks.

'It's okay, Erica. My name's Alice. I'm actually sixty-two, so it's quite a compliment.'

Philo coughs to cover up his laugh.

'Hi Philo.'

'Hello Alice.'

Erica looks from him to me, not happy we know each other.

I'm actually more hurt than I'm showing. I fucking hate needless bitchiness. But then, don't young people think everyone over thirty is old? Talk about a wake-up call.

Philo steps forward, takes my hand and kisses it.

'You must be the sexiest sixty-two-year-old on the whole planet, Alice'

'Thanks Philo. And you must be the filthiest man-child.'

He laughs. It's loud. Erica loops her arm through his, defensively, and glares at him.

'Anyway, we've got to grab some breakfast and get to band practice. Nice to see you, Elen. Bye.'

She turns on her heel, dragging her minions behind her.

Philo looks over his shoulder.

'Bye Alice. Nice boots!'

Erica yanks his arm, hard. They leave. Elen stares at me.

'What the fuck was that all about?'

'Female rivalry I think. It never seems to end. Just know that I am *never* going out with you again. I'm only fifteen years older than you and I get called your mother.'

'Erica is a bitch. She doesn't like girls.'

'Or old ladies, apparently.'

'Do you want me to go and punch the stupid cow? Little does she know Philo is already seeing someone else behind her back.'

'Jesus. That boy is a sociopath.'

'I know.'

My phone rings. I don't know the number and my phone doesn't recognise it. But it does seem vaguely familiar. Then I remember. Last night, several missed calls from Tommi and two from this number. I deleted the messages without listening. Is he trying to trick me again? A fucking model dressed as a sex worker just called me old. He really is picking the wrong time to annoy me. I take the call.

'Alice?'

The voice is familiar, but it's not Tommi.

'Alice, can you talk?'

'Harry?'

'Did you get my message yesterday?'

'Oh God, was that you? I accidentally deleted it. Where are you?'

'I'm in Soho. Can you get away from work and meet me?'

'There is no work, Harry. Your father-in-law just shut up shop.'

'What? Already?'

'Yup. So I'm free as a bird. But I can't afford to be jumping in cabs any more so can you give me half an hour? I'll get the

CHAPTER THIRTY-SIX

tube. I'm in Camden.'

'Of course. You want to meet at Red Café?'

'Okay. See you there.'

I look to Elen who is miserably finishing off her wine.

'Sorry Elen, I've got to go but I can meet you later.'

'You know what, Alice, I think I need to go to Noah's and put his pyjamas on and drink some wine.'

'You see! That's what I call a plan.'

She smiles a tiny smile.

'I'm sure he can find a way to soothe my sadness.'

'Oooh. Fucking the pain away?!'

'Alice!'

'Sorry, don't mind me. I'm just a dirty geriatric, aren't I?'

'Totally. Anyway, can we please talk this weekend? I'll probably be on Prozac by tomorrow afternoon.'

'Of course we can. I'll bet you find a job within the week anyway, but if not, sod it. Life's not for stressing. I'll call you at lunchtime tomorrow.'

'Thank you. Love you.'

Aww. Bless.

CHAPTER THIRTY-SEVEN

Harry looks like shit.

Well, not exactly shit. Just kind of rough. He's in jeans. I've never seen him in jeans. And a T-shirt; a muted blue thing. Plus he hasn't shaved and he's lost a bit of weight, which he didn't need to do, he suited his size. Now he looks more vulnerable. He's drinking black coffee. He stands when I reach the table and we hug. He feels leaner in my arms and smells of soap.

'What happened, Harry?'

He grimaces. We sit and he waves to the waitress. I order a cappuccino.

'Friday you were at work, Monday you were gone.'

'I ran off to a hotel in the Lakes.'

'Did you? Why? How come you didn't answer my texts?'

'I smashed my phone to pieces.'

'Eh?'

'Melissa was having one of her episodes. I decided to leave. Her father, knowing what she's like, tried to calm me down when I was packing on the Saturday morning. He Skyped me at her behest, the controlling little madam, but I told him I'd had it. He even offered to send us to the Bahamas for a month to get back "that honeymoon feeling". But I knew it wouldn't make any difference. I didn't want another second in her company. She wouldn't stop calling me when I was gone, so I stamped on my phone.'

'I didn't realise it was so bad. I thought you were just having a rough patch.'

'We've been having a rough patch since we got married.'

He laughs a dry laugh.

'I actually think the latest one was triggered by the fact I didn't seem so unhappy anymore. She just couldn't stand seeing me cheerful.'

'I'm sure that's not true.'

'It is. It obviously made her nervous.'

'Why are people such shits, Harry?'

He stares at me.

'God, I'm sorry Alice. You just lost your bloody job and I'm raving on about myself.'

'No, you're not.'

'Yes, I am. And you look so upset.'

'I'm not actually. I'm just exhausted.'

'From what?'

'All sorts.'

'Tell me about it.'

So I do. Over three coffees and a croissant. An hour of me, jabbering on. I tell him everything except details of my 'dalliances'. I just mention I've had a few drunken, meaningless encounters. Not that they were completely meaningless. Weirdly, they have helped build up my confidence and, in the case of Gracie, whose number I have carefully preserved in the back of my purse, there is a huge chance I might want to revisit the scene of the crime.

When I finish he looks shell-shocked and more than a little impressed.

'Your life is like a film. One of those horrendous, far-fetched ones that Melissa likes to moon over.'

'I can't imagine Melissa mooning over anything.'

'Well, her version of mooning, which is watching the film, fancying the lead man then spending the rest of the day questioning why I can't live up to him.'

'Nice.'

'Anyway, I don't envy you. As far as I can tell from what you just told me, you have outgrown Tommi. Simple as that. And if you didn't have Barney, you would have walked away a long time ago.'

' My beautiful Barney. Or my "problem" as you always so charmingly referred to him.'

'Oh, don't. Really, don't. That was so bad of me. I want kids, Alice. I love kids. I have two nieces that I adore. But Melissa was adamant that they were way down the list in our marriage, so I tried to persuade myself they weren't a priority for me either. Hence my harshness about your son. Please forgive me.'

'I'll think about it. Anyway, having a career outside the house and bringing up your child properly is a balancing act. You need to be a team if you have a partner and you have to make sacrifices. And in that context having kids is a "problem". You shouldn't do a job that makes your child a problem. That's the problem.'

'Right.'

'And to be honest, I don't want to be out all day, every day, doing a job that I haven't got the heart for.'

'Me neither. That's why I told my father-in-law I wouldn't

work for him anymore. Never has a job suited me less.'

'Is that why he closed the place down?'

'No. It was heading that way anyway. I think he tried harder than he usually would, with a business he'd lost interest in, just so that I'd have a job that pleased Melissa. Not that it did. When I left he didn't have to be bothered with it anymore.'

'Nice that he can treat life like a game of Monopoly.'

'Yes. But then he has his ridiculous daughter to deal with. So we all have our crosses to bear.'

Harry drags his seat noisily round and puts his arm around my shoulder.

'What a pair of losers we are.'

I chuckle.

'Are we just living in a world now where it's impossible to mate for life?'

'I don't have a clue. Having just run away from that loon, I'm not sure why people are so hell bent on finding "the one".'

'Me neither.'

'Well it sounds like you've been on a bit of a recce recently, to find the next one.'

'Shut up!'

I slap him. He laughs. Then another hand slaps me hard on the side of the head and we both spin in our seats.

Melissa, natural smoky tones that look like they were applied by a make-up artist, hair perfectly straight and shining like gold, simple woollen jacket and another pair of those bloody expensive jeans, is standing there, palm raised, eyes like Medusa, glaring at us both.

'I knew it! I knew it!'

He voice would shatter mirrors, it's so piercing. Her mouth twitches. My face throbs. If her palm had caught more of my ear than it did, the pressure of the blow would have broken my eardrum.

He stands as I jump up and yelp at her.

'What the *fuck?*'

She is quivering with righteous anger.

'I knew it was you! Stealing my husband, you fat old bitch.'

I rub my stinging head. Everyone is calling me old today.

'Oh my God, my ear.'

He looks at the side of my head.

'Are you okay?'

'I'll live.'

'Stop it! Stop asking if she's okay. I'm your wife, I'm your wife and I'm not okay, how dare you disappear. How dare you –'

She lifts her hands up as if to claw his face, but he steps forward and grabs her forearms.

His voice is calm but loaded. I've not heard him like this before.

'How did you know I was here?'

She screams in his face. He stands his ground, still holding her arms.

'I tracked you down at that hotel in the Lakes. An old friend of Dad's kept an eye on you. He got on the train when you did. He called me when you got here.'

'You got someone to follow me?'

'What else was I supposed to do?'

She's spitting as she shouts.

'You just went. You didn't say where. You're my husband. You can't just go away any time you feel like it.'

'I can do what I like Melissa. Anything I want. You may think you can buy anything but you don't own me.'

CHAPTER THIRTY-SEVEN

She begins to struggle again. I've moved off to a safe distance. This isn't my argument and she's actually given my head quite a crack.

'What about her? Is that it, the best you can do? It's an insult Harry, an insult to us. Look at her! You won't get a penny out of me if you file for divorce. I'll tell them you had an affair. I'll tell them!'

His voice gets calmer and slower. It has a mesmeric effect.

'Melissa, I do not want a single penny of your father's money. Because that's who it belongs to. You have never worked a stroke in your life. My own dad worked all his life. He has a lot of money, and if I went into the building trade tomorrow I would also have a lot of money.'

She sounds bewildered.

'A builder? You're not a builder.'

'That's where you're wrong, Melissa. Education or not, that's what I'm best at. And I don't want a single tie to you or your family. I want out, lock stock. So there's absolutely nothing you can hold over me. As for Alice, she could ring the police now and have you arrested. I am a witness to an assault and Daddy couldn't buy you out of that one, could he? Do you want to do that, Alice?'

I kind of do actually. I look her in the eye.

'I should. There's something wrong with you.'

She sneers. 'You have done everything you can to get him. Look at you. It's pathetic.'

Harry is now virtually growling. 'I am not having an affair with Alice. I was comforting her when you walked in, because she's my friend.'

He then gets close enough to her face to feel her breath.

'But I'll tell you this, Melissa. Alice has more beauty and

class than you'll ever have. You are rotten inside and what's more you are totally joyless. You can try every trick in the book to stop me divorcing you, but it won't work because nothing you do will make me care. Leaving you is the biggest relief of my life. Take the money and stick it.'

She tries to hold him, her face contorting.

'Harry, please. Get rid of her, let's talk alone. We can make this work.'

He takes my arm, shaking her off.

'Come on, Alice. You have an assault to report.'

Melissa's face is a picture. Her voice becomes a screech.

'They won't believe you!'

'Excuse me.'

The waitress is pretending to clean a table. Harry is sweet and polite towards her. She looks up.

'Did you see what happened here?'

'Yes. That blonde lady walked up behind the other lady, out of nowhere, and smacked her across the head.'

Melissa is looking more and more like a cornered rat. She has major red blotches on her neck.

'If I report it to the police, would you be a witness? I'd have to take your number.'

She smiles. 'Of course.'

'That's very nice of you.'

Melissa looks ready to foam at the mouth. Before we can leave, she suddenly runs. Harry shouts after her.

'I'll be calling your father to tell him you had me followed!'

After she slams the door behind her, Harry smiles again at the waitress.

'Thanks again. Can we find you here if we need you?'

'Week days you can. My name's Leigh. Is she mental or

CHAPTER THIRTY-SEVEN

something? Is your head okay?'

I take out my hand mirror and check out the damage. I've got a lump forming. She must have caught me with her ring.

'Yes, thanks. More shock than anything else.'

Harry looks again at my head.

'I can't believe this has happened. She had me followed, for Christ's sake. Thank you for your help Leigh. I'm Harry. This is Alice.'

As we vacate the premises, I realise I feel a little queasy. The past few days have been a bit too much and getting walloped across the head is just the icing on the cake.

'Alice, I'm so sorry. She is out of control.'

'Has she ever hit you like that?'

'No comment.'

We walk down the street together towards the tube station. Wow. The world is screwed up.

'Are you really going to call her dad?'

'I'll have to. She's gone too far this time. I'm not sure Charles will have sanctioned her having me followed. He's actually all right really, just a bit vain and grand sometimes, and he knows she's a nightmare.'

I lean against a wall, feeling unsteady.

'Are you okay?'

'Yeah. It's just the shock of being hit. I don't like violence.'

'Me neither. Would you like me to take you to the police station? It would be good for her to feel the consequences of her actions for once.'

'Right now, I want to go home and curl up in bed. Just for a few hours before I get Barney.'

He puts his arm around me and supports me as I walk.

'You didn't deserve what you got in there. I'm so sorry.'

'Harry, we both know we're not totally innocent in this. We did something naughty while you guys were still together. I can't really blame her. Women pick up on this stuff. Well, women who aren't me, I didn't pick up on what Tommi was doing for a whole year!'

'She should have hit me, not you.'

I stop and look up at him.

'Harry, can we be mates and stuff after what happened between us, or will it be too weird? Because I really like talking to you but my life's so up in the air right now; other complications would just totally scramble what's left of my brain.'

He holds up his hand.

'After what you've told me today, I think you are the very last person in the world who needs to be "getting involved" with anyone. Least of all me. I don't even know what I'm doing next week. I might go and work for my dad. I might go off around the world for a year. The world is my lobster!'

I nod and smile. I'm so glad for him, escaping that horrible marriage. But I'm also unaccountably sad. I can't just run off. Being a grown-up really can be rubbish sometimes.

CHAPTER THIRTY-EIGHT

I had no idea that Spain could be so hot at this time of year. While the freezing rain pours down in London, I sit by the pool in front of my spa hotel, which was extremely reasonably priced, and read the worst book I have ever clapped eyes on. I can't believe that something so sickly could be a bestseller. This will be my first and last foray into reading 'romantic' books, I can tell you that. After what I've just been through I don't believe in romance any more.

Mum is currently staying at my house. She's working her way through every Catherine Cookson DVD she can find, while Barney is out being educated or asleep at night. She is also making his breakfast, taking him to school, picking him up in the afternoon, cooking his dinner and, I'm sure, generally spoiling him to death – the biggest irony being, he isn't giving her a second's trouble when putting on his uniform in the morning, the little rotter.

Every night at seven we have a Skype conversation, Barney and I. He's bouncing off the walls at the minute because we've decided to go off on holiday with my parents the day after Christmas. Even my dad, who hates the cold weather, has been lured away by the promise of sunshine in December.

I'm only here because my mum is a bloody hero. When I got home on Friday night and told her I wouldn't be going out with Tommi after all, then explained about his relationship with Emma and his 'dalliance' before Barney was born, she surprised the life out of me. I hadn't even vaguely accounted for the vehemence of my mother's hatred of 'affairs'. When I told her he'd been sleeping with someone else for a whole year, I thought her perm was going to explode off her head.

She got a steely look in her eye and told me that we could all keep Barney happy and well adjusted as a family, as long as we worked together, and that I couldn't stay with a man with the 'morals of a stray dog'.

I'd better never let her know what I've been getting up to lately, then.

She said I shouldn't disturb Barney's schooling but that I needed a break, what with me becoming unemployed and having to put our house on the market. (Tommi is insisting he wants his half of the house value ASAP.) She told me to book flights and a hotel immediately and that she would hold the fort. I couldn't have been more grateful, as I've had a lot to think about.

My text inbox since then has been an absolute riot. Highlights include:

WHY DID YOU TELL HIM I TOLD YOU? He is now dating Lorraine. My life is over.

This from a rather overwrought Emma two days after Tommi walked out of the house. Two days. He will never learn, apparently, and is now staying with the receptionist with the giant hoop earrings. His mother is outraged, but making excuses for him. Why am I not surprised? He just needs someone to adore him, I think, and he'll get bored again

CHAPTER THIRTY-EIGHT

soon enough. The stupid thing is that he does love Barney and me. As for Emma, she'll get over it. Eventually. In about fifty years, the bloody nut.

Beautiful Alice. Get over here. Lemon Meringue Martinis and many kisses are yours for the taking, you sexy mutha. Gxx

I texted Gracie when I was tipsy in my hotel room. That was her reply.

I'm going to Australia for six months with Noah! So excited, Cocktails next week? Xx

Elen has finally decided to be young and carefree which makes me very happy.

The spare room is ready for you and my godson. Come and drink wine, we'll take care of you. We both love you lots. S x o

I think Suze is starting to get it. Bless her.

Alice, I love you. Please call me. I'm lost without you. Txxxxxxx
You have broken me. Call, please x
Why are you so being so cold? It's evil.
You have no soul
I miss you. Barney needs us together
Sell the house right now. I have nothing because of you.
Have you seen the charger for my laptop?

Tommi must be having an early mid-life crisis, it's the only explanation. He probably sent most of these from Lorraine's bed while drunk. There are another seventeen of them. I have to try to find humour in the situation, because he's Barney's dad and therefore won't be exiting my life any time soon. Eventually when he gets over himself maybe we can be mates again. His mum calls me every day and he's a mummy's boy so I'm sure it'll be fine. How did I last all of that time with him? I have no clue.

I am very sorry for your inconvenience at the closing of Benham Design. I trust you are satisfied with the full and final settlement after such a traumatic episode and apologise for any inconvenience. I wish you good luck with your future endeavours. Yours, Charles Benham.

This actually came from Mr Benham's lawyer's telephone the day I landed at Palma airport. When I checked with my bank he'd deposited three years wages into my account. Three years. I was nearly sick with relief. This has to be a payoff for Melissa clipping me around the ear. I called the lawyer to make sure it wasn't a mistake. He said it wasn't. I said to give Mr Benham my regards. He said he would.

Suddenly I'm not skint and not in desperate need of another job that will take me away from my son. Part-time will be fine. I can rent a place for two years and still have enough left for a deposit on a flat. Once we sell our monstrosity of a house I shall have plenty of savings. I can't wait to tell my mother. I shall keep it as a surprise for when I get back tomorrow.

And, this last text came at eight o'clock this morning:

Business proposition if you're up for it. WHERE ARE YOU? H x

I called him straight away and when I told him where I was he said he could fly out for a meeting today. After three days alone, I thought why not? I'm not leaving until tomorrow

CHAPTER THIRTY-EIGHT

morning. It would be nice to have lunch with another human being instead of on my own with a shoddy book.

I'm actually missing Barney really badly. After the three Skype conversations we've had, I've been very sad. I'm not really suited to being away from him, it seems. But at least I know now. All of that daydreaming about running away to the sun and the sea was all fantasy. I miss Barney's spindle-armed hugs and his boy-smell neck. A night off here and there is fine, a bit of fun that I can come home from. But I have finally accepted the fact I don't want to pretend to be a twenty-four-year-old on a singles beach holiday. I'm a mother with a beautiful son and, mostly, where I go I want him to be. And there's nothing wrong with that.

Of course, when he's off having fun with Daddy, or his grandparents, this mummy is allowed to have her fun, too, any way she sees fit and I couldn't give a shit what anybody thinks of that.

Speaking of fit, Harry will be here in less than an hour. I need to shower. I smell of chlorine from the pool and my hair's a mess.

CHAPTER THIRTY-NINE

Harry really has changed in a few weeks. In his long shorts and black-vest top, with his stubble and newly cropped hair he looks like a different man. More relaxed. Definitely less uptight.

We've got a very cold half-empty bottle of white in a bucket on the table and the seafood sharing platter is almost done. It feels extremely strange, him sitting opposite me at this table as the sea breaks on the shore thirty feet away and the sun beats down on the sleepy sunbathers.

His proposal is very simple. His dad wants to step back from the business as he's getting older now, but doesn't want to jack it in completely. Since Harry arrived home and announced the end of his marriage and his wish to 'start again' in the building trade, his dad quickly went from sceptical to excited. He wants Harry to start looking for rundown properties in London to buy at auction and make into desirable homes to sell or keep as rental properties. Harry will coordinate building work and all of that side, with the help of his dad. The money to be earned can be quite substantial. He wonders if I'd like to come on board as an interior designer. He thinks I have a good eye and it will be my job to make the interiors interesting and get

CHAPTER THIRTY-NINE

them to a high standard as cheaply as possible. This will mean cleverly sourcing materials and a lot of recycling.

Basically, my dream job.

If anything 'goes wrong' or any of us aren't happy then that will be that. No more working together. I am gobsmacked. I actually can't think of anything I'd rather do.

'Harry, I'd love it.'

'Look, this is a new venture so we'd have to learn as we go and liaise about everything, but my dad knows his onions and I think he'd love a weekly train journey to the smoke. Give him a new lease of life. He wants to invest in me and I think he's over the moon I'm going to carry on in the family trade. Not that he'd say as much. He's a man of few words.'

'Well, if he were here right now, I'd kiss him.'

'I'm here right now.'

He's wearing sunglasses so I can't see his eyes but I shake my fist at him and shoot him a look.

'Oy. That's no way to run a business.'

He smiles at me.

'So, how you been doing all on your lonesome? Three days, you said?'

'Yes. Home tomorrow. Can't wait to see Barney.'

'I'll bet.'

'Can I ask something?'

'Of course.'

'What the hell did you say to Charles Benham? My payoff was a bit heftier than expected.'

He chuckles.

'No really, a lot heftier.'

'How much heftier?'

'Three years' worth of wages heftier.'

He whistles.

'Nice. Hope you're not going to spend it all on Uggs.'

'As if! I'm a flip-flops girl recently, didn't you notice?'

I hold up a foot bedecked with my new pink, sparkly sandal.

'Lovely. Very demure. Not.'

'So what did you tell him?'

'He's American, Alice. Americans get sued for anything and everything. I just told him that Melissa had assaulted you in public and there was a witness. I said a large welt had appeared on your head and if you went to the police, Melissa would be in a lot of trouble. On top of that, you could sue her. For the first time, in all of the years I've known him, Charles sounded flustered. He asked what you were going to do. I said I thought you weren't going to do anything. But, I said, seeing as you were on the brink of being a single mother, maybe he could thank you with a slightly larger pay-out for losing your job. Looks like he did just that. I told you he was decent.'

'It's amazing. Seeing as I kind of deserved the smack around the head.'

He takes off his glasses and stares at me.

'Are you insane? You deserved nothing of the sort. If anyone deserved a smack it was me. And she's given me plenty of those over the last two years so I think we're all quits, don't you?'

We chat about family after that and how much life can take you by surprise. In fact we chat for so long that when Harry eventually looks at his watch it is almost dinnertime and we've polished off two bottles of wine. His flight back is at ten p.m. and he's left his bag at my hotel so we decide to head back. It's only fifteen minutes' walk and as we stroll and chat I realise that much as coming away alone has been liberating, it's very nice to have a friend by my side. On the way we buy ice creams and suddenly I laugh.

'What's up?'

'Do you know how mad it is that you flew out here for a day-trip? We could have had this meeting when I got back, you know.'

'What, in a rainy cafe, in the freezing bloody cold? This is much better. It was a total excuse to come to the sunshine. A little treat to myself.'

'We should always treat ourselves, shouldn't we?'

He gives me the naughtiest of glances. I look away. We're just about to work together. You can't work with someone and be naughty with them too. It causes trouble.

We take the lift to my room, where Harry has left his hand bag. I open the balcony doors and look out over the sea. The breeze is delicious.

'I have an hour before I get a cab to the airport. Should we have a last drink on your balcony? Then I'll grab the quickest of showers if that's okay?'

'Of course.'

I'm now a little tongue-tied. I bustle to the mini-bar and take out the bottle of champagne that Harry brought me earlier as a 'hello' present.

As I open it, the light, long drapes by the balcony window swish in the breeze. As does my long, thin beach dress. The sun and the dress remind me of another beach holiday, many moons ago, with a beautiful surf instructor called Gene. It makes me smile.

My dress is cream coloured and semi-transparent so I'm wearing a red tankini underneath it. Harry is washing his face with cold water. When he comes out of the bathroom I am already pouring the champagne.

'I remember last time we drank champagne.'

'Harry. No.'

'What?'

I hold out a tumbler of the fizzing liquid towards him.

'We are about to work together. We can't… you know.'

He takes the glass and I turn to pick up the other. As I do he moves in close behind me and wraps his free hand around my waist, resting it on my belly button as he hugs me from behind. My voice becomes a little less authoritative as he burrows in and kisses my neck through my hair.

'Harry, this isn't allowed.'

I hear him placing the glass down beside him as his other hand snakes around my ribcage. Immediately my body mutinies and I arch back into him.

'We can't work side by side and also do this. It'll end in disaster.'

His hands move upwards until he is holding both of my breasts through the sheer dress and the tankini. I try not to make a sound. He puts his mouth to my ear.

'Why don't we count this as a treat to ourselves?'

One of his hands works its way down and nestles itself between my legs. The heat is instant.

'We're not getting married. We're just finishing what we started. Just this once.'

I'm now finding it hard to say anything at all. Before me is the dressing table with a hairdryer, room menu and mirror. I lean forward onto my hands, pushing my backside against him, feeling the hardness in his shorts. He bends and picks up the hem of my dress. Slowly he raises it until he reaches my bikini pants. Hooking his thumbs into the sides he lowers them, until

CHAPTER THIRTY-NINE

he can see my bare bottom through the sheer material and my pants are on the floor. As I lightly step out of them, he raises my hem once again until it's resting on my waist and I am exposed to him. He bends and kisses an exposed cheek, then I hear his zip lowering. From behind he slips his hands over my breasts and all at once he has pushed himself inside me.

He begins to move against me, gently at first then adds his right hand to the equation, fingering, as his thrusts become more insistent.

Oh God, it feels so good, I could come right now. I want to come right now. I will... I will...

But he stops. Stops before he loses himself and just before I do too.

This newly confident, newly passionate Harry turns me, ripping the dress and tankini top over my head and drops his own shorts, leaving only his unbuttoned white shirt. His kiss is deep.

'If this is my one off treat, I'm going to savour it.'

I'm not sure he's going to make his flight tonight. And I'm not sure I should be fucking this man. I'm not sure if I'm going to visit Gracie on the weekend after I get back. I'm not sure the interior design thing will work out. I'm not sure it won't get too heavy once we've shagged. I'm not sure how anything works anymore and I'm not sure if I even care.

I'm only sure that Barney will never know of my secret adventures and I will never make him feel second best.

And I'm sure, as I fall back on the clean white sheets, that what's happening now feels fantastic and free and isn't hurting anyone. And that, for now, is good enough for me.

Printed in Dunstable, United Kingdom